Friend of the Undead

My Life Among the Undead:
Book 1

Camara M. Bragdon

DEDICATION

I dedicate this book to my high school English teacher, Mr. William Prest, whose 500-word essays opened the portal to my writing career.

CHAPTERS

Chapter 1:
I Go to an Art Gallery with a Vampire

I woke up to the sound of my alarm clock going off with a loud beep, beep. I shielded my eyes from the red glare of the digital numbers. 6:30 a.m. I hit the snooze button and lay in bed for another five minutes. "Crap!" I muttered to myself two minutes later, realizing that I wasn't going back to sleep anytime soon. I threw back the covers and shuffled to the shower to get ready for work.

As I ate a fancy breakfast of bagels with cream cheese, I glanced at my stack of three paintings standing up by the front door. I had worked on them for two weeks. One showed two baby mermaids chasing after a baby dolphin. The second painting was a unicorn mother licking her foal. The third one was of my centaur friend, Creighton Horsefeathers, getting pelted with snowballs by her niece and nephew.

I made a mental note to call Robin about dropping off my artwork at the Zephyr Art Gallery. Between working his way up the Zephyr Police Department's career ladder and putting together his band, my brother barely had time to help out his younger sister, the soon-to-be-famous Shelly Anderson, with her aspiring art career. I grabbed my cell phone and dI grabbed my cell phone and dialed Robin's number. He answered on the fifth ring.

"Hello?" came a groggy answer.

"Hey, bro!" I chirped as I headed out my door. "I just wanted to remind you about dropping off my paintings at the art gallery."

I heard Robin mumble something about annoying sisters who interrupted his beauty sleep. "Shelly, you woke me up to tell me that?"

"Hey, I wanted to make sure you didn't forget."

"I didn't. Good-bye!"

I stared at the cell phone as if I could make itself to redial. Unfortunately, I can't telepathically communicate with inanimate objects. There are times when I had a better superpower. As I have learned these past few years in Zephyr, when humans enter this magical world, they each acquire one superpower that suggests something of their personality or hobby. My dad, Timothy Anderson, for instance, can stretch his body into any possible position without hurting himself, which can look really gross sometimes.

My mom had died in a car accident when my brother and I were just entering the eighth grade. Dad listened to us slaughter the Spanish language for a class, helped through dreaded science fairs, and sent us money when we were at college. Dad's powers come in very handy during busy nights at the diner he owns. I gathered up my purse and lunch and was out the door at eight o'clock on the dot.

I walked down to the beautiful two-story library with the marble edifice, where I am an assistant librarian. When I arrived in the staff room, I saw my friend, Cricket Lunesta, putting her lunch in her locker.

"Hey, girl!" the fairy replied. Cricket is a great friend. One look at her and a stranger might think that behind her light green moth-like wings, and her two beige, feathery antennae is a quiet woman in her early twenties. But Cricket is the loudest among my circle of friends. "So, are you ready for the big night?"

I shrugged as I set my stuff on the floor right up against the row of puke green lockers. "Guess so." I reached up with my locker key and wiggled it around in the lock of my top locker. My locker is so old that I have to turn the key several times to lock and unlock it. I heaved my purse and my green canvas bag that held the latest book I was reading, my handy umbrella, and my lunch bag up into my locker.

Then I headed to the circulation desk where my supervisor, a werewolf by the name of Raquel Lupus, was already halfway done with stamping the due date slips for the next day. In her human form, Raquel is a lovely woman with olive skin and long black hair that was now pushed behind her tufted ears. As with all werewolves, Raquel has one magical ability: superhuman speed, which becomes apparent when she turns into a werewolf. Think of the original *Wolf Man* movies, but without the tearing off of clothes and communicating only in grunts and growls. "So, are your paintings all set for tonight?"

she asked me.

"No, the gallery is not opened until eleven, but Robin is supposed to drop off the paintings during lunch."

Raquel smiled at me. I knew what she was thinking. That's my magical power—I can read the minds of the undead and telepathically communicate with them. Technically speaking, Weres aren't undead, but they do fall into that category because the change only happens at night. "No, Raquel, don't have Halifax remind Robin," I said with a grin. Raquel's werewolf husband has superhuman strength. Even in his human form, the police detective is six times as strong as the normal man. Halifax is a nice guy, but his six-foot-five muscular frame can be a little bit intimidating, especially to my brother.

My day was uneventful until a mysterious elf walked up to me while I was putting books away. Now elves in Zephyr are just like humans except that they have pointed ears, so I was surprised when he came up so quietly that I barely heard his breathing. Even though Zephyr is a magical city, we do get our share of creeps, especially at the library. He wore a black hood over his head that pulled down over his face. "Miss Anderson?"

he asked in a low, scary voice.

"Yes?" I replied. I wasn't wearing any kind of nametag. So,

unless, he knew me from the diner or my neighborhood, this guy

was bordering on the creepy stalker edge of reality.

"You friends with Eddie Van Helsing?" asked Mr.

Faceless.

"Yeah," I replied hesitantly, not sure how he knew this fact

or why he would care that Eddie is one of my best friends.

"Tell him that the Chairman wants it by tonight at the

gallery." With that cryptic message, the elf turned away and

left me alone with the beginning of a mystery and a creepy

feeling slowly settling in the pit of my stomach.

The sun had started to set when I arrived home. I sighed

with relief as I saw that my artwork was gone. Robin had

dropped them off. Or he had Dad or his friend and roommate,

the satyr Strider Hornsby, do it. The little slacker! I changed out

of my work clothes and put on a navy blue cocktail dress that I

had bought a couple of weeks ago. As I was putting on makeup (a rare occurrence in my life), I heard a knock on my front door.

"Shelly, it's Eddie!"

"It's open!" I shouted.

My front door opened, and a vampire with curly black hair crossed my threshold. Eddie Van Helsing looks to be about twenty-five, but, of course, bitten vampires don't age, so who knows how old he is. "Are you almost ready?" he asked impatiently.

I poked my head around the bathroom door. "You just got here, and anyway, the showing isn't until seven. Help yourself to anything in the fridge!" I went back to slapping on lipstick. I heard Eddie open the refrigerator door. Because he is a vegetarian (he can't drink blood for medical reasons as he has yet to explain to me), I always keep a couple bottles of vegetable juice in the fridge for him. I heard a glass of liquid being poured. "Did you sleep well today?" I asked.

"Yeah, I guess so."

I detected a note of nervousness in Eddie's voice. I could have read his mind, but that would have been rude. So I decided to be more direct. "Is everything all right, Eddie? You seem a little jumpy tonight."

"I'm fine. Are you almost ready to go?" He came into the bathroom. The vampire was wearing a navy blue suit with a light pink tie that went remarkably well with his pale skin. He looked fine, very fine, indeed. He smiled a nervous smile, showing his two curved fangs. "You look nice."

I looked at him, unsure whether it was a sincere compliment or a diversion from what was really going on with him. The minute I began to read his mind, he blocked it off. Vampires are the only members of the undead community who can block telepathy. I believe that it might have something to do with their ability to shapeshift into either mist or a nocturnal animal. Eddie never blocked out my mind-reading, not without telling me first.

He grabbed my wrist and pulled me towards the front door. "Come on, let's go!" he said.

I planted my feet firmly to the tile floor. "Hey, slow down, Paco!" Eddie knew better than to push me around, and he let go of me. Screw the fact that he was twice as strong as the average man. I placed my hands on my hips. "What is going on?" I demanded.

The vampire looked at me with his deep green eyes. "Nothing! I'm just nervous. For you, that is."

I grabbed my black purse and headed out the door with Eddie right behind me. We stepped out into the fresh night air. The Zephyr sun had just finished its descent into the horizon. I smiled as I noticed the car that my fanged escort had brought. "Hey, you brought the picklemobile!" I said brightly. Indeed, the beat-up looking vehicle was in the shape of a dark green cucumber equipped with two doors on each side. Cars in Zephyr are considered a rare commodity. Most people use giant insects, winged horses, dragons, or unicorns. My friend builds various vehicles, and all of them in shapes of fruits and vegetables.

Eddie grinned at me. "It's a cucumber!" he corrected as he opened the passenger door for me.

"Pickle. It even smells like a pickle." I held my nose to block out the overpowering smell of pickle juice. "What are you using for fuel? Fermented juice? It stinks!"

Eddie eased into the bright green leather driver's seat and

touched the smiling cucumber air freshener that was dangling from the rearview mirror. "Gift from my Aunt Phoebe," he explained.

That explained it. "The Countess has unique gift ideas," I said as I buckled my seatbelt. Before he became a vampire, one of Eddie's many jobs was driving race cars. In fact, he has a pretty impressive resume—including a stint as a spy, professional bounty hunter, and superior mechanical skills. The list goes on. I still have yet to figure out why he is working as a soda jerk/ bouncer in my dad's diner. Maybe he wanted a job where he wouldn't get shot at. "So, how many vampire babes have you picked up in this snazzy machine?"

Eddie started up the engine and pulled out of my driveway. He smirked at me. "Witty!" he replied.

It was quiet for a few minutes as we drove to the gallery. I decided to try to read Eddie's mind to figure out why he was so jumpy. But every time I attempted to enter his mind, he would block my mind reading. So I tried another approach. "Are you hungry? Because there's a sandwich drive-thru on your left."

Eddie gave a non-committal shrug and pulled into Mac's

Place. He did not order anything, but since I was starving, I ordered a chicken Caesar wrap. His hands shook as he took my money. I had never seen my friend act this way before. I finally gave up, trying to read his mind. If Eddie wanted to tell me what was going on, he would do so in his own good time.

Once we arrived at the parking lot of the art gallery, I carefully ate my sandwich. The last thing I needed was a massive glob of mayo on my lap. I noticed that Eddie's eyes were sweeping the parking lot as if he were looking for someone. Then I remembered what happened at the library. "Eddie, do you know anyone by the name of 'the Chairman?'" I asked him, waking him out of his trance.

He jumped as if I had poked him with a pin. "No—who's asking?" he snapped.

"Whoa!" I held up my hands. "Someone certainly woke up on the wrong side of the coffin." Eddie rolled his eyes. "Look, I was shelving today, and this elf came up to me asking if I was Miss Anderson."

"What did you tell him?"

"I told him yes. Dumb question, Eddie. Why would I lie about who I was? Then he asked me if you and I were friends."

"What did you say?"

"Yes. And then the guy said that the Chairman wants it here tonight." I paused in my narrative. "Eddie, what is going on?" I asked.

"Nothing." He checked his watch. "Look at the time. It's almost sixty-thirty." He got out of the car and walked around to my side. He threw open my door, and barely gave me enough time to grab my purse before he dragged me up the stairs by my wrist.

"You're not acting very gentlemanlike," I growled as I wrenched myself free of his grip. I ran my fingers through my hair and smoothed down my dress.

"I'm sorry, Shelly," my vampire friend apologized. "I've just been a little bit jumpy lately."

"Yeah, about as jumpy as a rabbit on Ritalin," I retorted. This time I was the one to grab Eddie by the elbow. "How about we let it go?" I suggested. I tossed my head to one side. "Let's make our entrance look good."

It looked like all of my family and friends were inside the gallery. I made my way to my table that was in the back corner of the large blue ballroom. My paintings were resting against the wall. Eddie had begun to help me set them up when he suddenly lost his grip on my artwork of the silver unicorn. It would have hit the floor had it not been for the arm that had literally stretched out and caught the corner of the painting.

"Easy on my daughter's paintings, Eddie," my dad admonished as he walked four feet to where the vampire was standing. My dad was wearing a brown suit coat over a black shirt and chocolate brown dress pants. "She spent a lot of time on them."

"Sorry, Mr. Anderson," Eddie apologized as he and Dad set the painting to where I was indicating with my index finger.

"Oh, sweetie, I got something for you," Dad said to me. "It's out with Tradewinds. Come on. I'll show you."

I turned to my date, nervously tapping the carpet with his foot. "I'll be right back, Eddie."

Eddie shook himself out of his trance. "Yeah, sure, I'll

make sure that nothing happens to your artwork."

Dad and I walked out to the parking lot, where I saw his giant golden eagle, Tradewinds, preening himself. Dad stretched out his arm to the other side of the bird's saddle and produced a bouquet of rainbow-colored roses. "Congratulations, Shelly," he said, "Mom would have been very proud of you." Dad gave me a big hug.

"I hope everything goes well tonight. Hey, where's Amelia?" I asked Dad about his girlfriend. Amelia Cross was a human who had come into Zephyr a few months before we did. She had the power to move inanimate objects. Dad had been dating her for almost two years. She was perfect for Dad, and Robin and I really liked her.

"She wanted to come with me, but someone needed to run the diner. So, she insisted that I go."

"Tell her thanks. Did she help you pick out the flowers?"

"She did," Dad replied with a broad, dreamy smile. He had started smiling like that again the day he met Amelia.

"Well," I said, "I nearly went into cardiac arrest when Eddie nearly dropped my paintings."

"Speaking of Eddie, is something wrong with him?"

"I don't know, Dad," I said as we walked back inside. "I've tried asking him, but he keeps on avoiding the issue or whatever it is."

"What about reading his mind?"

"I've tried that. He blocks me out every time."

"Hmm," Dad murmured as if he was looking for an answer, but he did not find one. Pausing for a moment, he said, "Well, Eddie knows that he can always come to me if he's in any trouble."

By the time we had arrived back inside, I had spotted Robin and his friend, Strider Hornsby, walking towards us. Dad went off to chat with a couple of his friends. "Hey, Shelly," twenty-seven-year-old Strider asked, his squirrel grey Rasta cap covering his two curved horns that were in the midst of his shoulder-length black hair. I wondered who dressed the satyr because the hat didn't even come close to complimenting his black, tieless suit. "What's up with Eddie? Can we say paranoid?"

"What do you mean?" I asked my brother's half-human,

half-goat friend.

"This weird elf walked up to Eddie and started talking to him. Eddie looked really nervous."

"What did this elf look like?"

"He was all in black and had a hood pulled over his face," Robin replied. "He looked really suspicious." My brother was wearing his blue police uniform, off-duty, I might add (I swear, he must sleep in it) and was in full cop mode. Dad says that it will wear off after a few more months on the job. He pushed up the black and navy cap that was covering his short auburn hair. "Hey, nice flowers. From Eddie?"

I shook my head. "No, from Dad."

"You wish they were from Eddie."

I got back to the issue. "Eddie's been acting weird all night. And yes, I did try reading his mind, but he keeps on blocking my attempts." I glanced past Robin and Strider, but there was no one at my table. "Where's Eddie?"

Chapter 2:
Eddie and I Have Our First Big Fight

Robin and Strider looked at my exhibit. Suddenly, it felt like spiders were running up and down my spine. Something was not right. I began to concentrate on seeing if I could find the vampire by locating his brain waves. We heard some commotion coming from a nearby hallway.

By the time we entered the hallway, Eddie had pinned the elf that I had seen earlier up against the wall. The elf's hood was down, showing his greasy hair. Etched upon his neck was a massive skull with blood dripping out of an eye socket and a black viper slithering out of the other one. No doubt, the rest of his body had many more pretty tattoos. For the first time, I actually studied his face. When I saw his greenish-yellow eyes, a shiver ran up my spine. His scruffy five o'clock shadow made a poor attempt at hiding an S-shaped scar along his left jawline. What had Eddie gotten himself into?

"Get out of here!" Eddie growled at the man, his green eyes narrowing. He evidently knew that the guy was trouble, but wasn't about to tell anyone why.

"Is there a problem?" Robin asked, reaching for his badge. He pulled it out to further prove his authenticity as the law.

The minute Robin spoke, the vampire let go of the elf.

"No, officer," the elf replied as he picked himself, "just a case of mistaken identity." He glared at Eddie with his piercing yellow eyes. "You'll regret this!" He turned away and disappeared into the crowd.

I looked at Eddie. "Are you okay?"

Eddie nodded as he straightened his collar and tie. "Like the guy said. Just a case of mistaken identity. He thought I was someone else." It did not take a mind reader to know that he was lying. I thought about reading his mind, but I knew that he would just block my attempts again. Instead, he changed the

18

subject. "So, has anyone given you a price on your paintings?"

Now I remembered why I was at the art gallery. "No, but I hardly think that my paintings will sell for tons of money."

Robin looked at my roses. A purple and pink striped one was wilting already. He touched it, and suddenly it sprang back to full bloom. That was Robin's magical talent: control of plants. "Did Dad water these?" he asked me.

"I'm sure he did, Robin," I replied. Because he was the one closest to me, I thrust the roses in my brother's hands the moment I saw the dwarf, Samuel Hedge, looking at my paintings. I began to flag down the renowned art critic. He was almost four feet tall and had a mop of red hair that complemented his forest green three-piece suit. "Mr. Hedge!" I began to trot over to him, thanking myself that I do not wear high heels. "I'm Michelle Anderson," I said in between attempts to catch my breath, "I spoke with your secretary about my art exhibit." I only use my full name professionally.

"Oh, yes," he said as if a light of recognition went on all over his head. For a long, nerve-racking fifteen minutes, the dwarf looked at all three of my paintings, cocking his head to one side or taking off his black glasses and peering down at every little detail, right down to each point on each blade of grass. Finally, he spoke, "Well, Miss Anderson, this artwork is awe-inspiring. The facial details on the little centaurs are very realistic. I can almost hear them laughing."

"Thank you, sir," I replied.

"So how much are the paintings worth?" Eddie blurted out without thinking.

I shot the vampire with a dirty look. *Eddie!* I telepathically scolded him, *shut up!* Why he would care was, once again, beyond me. Then I turned to Mr. Hedge. "I'm so sorry, sir. My friend doesn't think before he speaks."

Mr. Hedge gave a non-committal nod. "I'd say that if you were selling them, you'd get about one-fifty for each painting."

"Actually, I wasn't planning on selling them. I just wanted a price evaluation."

By the crestfallen look on Eddie's face, I could tell that something had upset him. "I'll be out in the car," he said to me in a quiet voice.

I shrugged. I watched the vampire walk out the large

double doors, and then I turned back to Mr. Hedge. "I'm really sorry about my friend," I apologized once again. Actually, I was glad that Eddie had left the building. Any more outbursts and I would have held the world record for the most apologies in one night. And probably would have driven a wooden stake threw Eddie's heart. "He's not been himself lately."

Mr. Hedge gave me an understanding smile. "As I was saying, Miss Anderson, your artwork is very heart-warming. You really get to the heart of what life here in Zephyr is really like. If you ever decide to sell, I have no doubt that your artwork will be trendy."

I merely smiled. If I said anything, I would have completely screwed up the moment. I think that is why Eddie and I are such good friends. We both have an open-mouth-insert-foot disease.

After being corralled by friends congratulating me, I finally made it out to the picklemobile with my three paintings. Eddie was in a very animated conversation on his cell phone, but I could tell that it was not the best one he ever had. I set the paintings on the pavement. Demons took over my soul, and I gave two sharp raps on the passenger window.

If Eddie were not jumpy earlier this evening, he was now. The vampire dropped his cell phone. He reached across the seat and unlocked my door. "That wasn't funny, Shelly!"

I had to stop laughing to speak to my friend. "Oh, the look on your face was priceless, Eddie." I was trying to balance my artwork in my hands and keep the door open with my foot. I finally put the paintings in the backseat. "If only I had a camera!" I said, climbing into the passenger seat.

The vampire only grimaced at me. Apparently, my little joke did not go over very well. He picked up his cell phone from the spotless car floor and placed it on the seat between us. He started up the car and was pulling out of the parking lot when he asked what else Mr. Hedge had to say.

"He really likes my artwork and thinks it has a lot of potential." I casually twisted the handle of my purse. Even though I was really excited about showing off what I considered masterpieces, I was more concerned about Eddie's nervousness. This was not like him.

His cell phone started ringing, and I glanced down to see who it was. (Okay, I'll admit that I'm just a tad bit nosy.)The number on the caller ID was blocked.

Eddie snatched up the phone and pressed a button, immediately sending the call to voicemail. He clearly knew who it was, but didn't want to divulge the information.

This was getting on my nerves. I decided to ask him directly. "Eddie, what's going on?"

"Nothing! Why are you pestering me with these questions? Look, I said I don't want to talk about it, so don't ask me!" he snapped. He glanced away from the road and shook his index finger in my face. "And don't even try to read my mind. It's a violation of my privacy!"

I snorted. "When have you ever cared about your privacy?" Eddie was the one who had taught me how to read the minds of the undead and how to telecommunicate with them. I did not wait for an answer. "I'm worried about you. You've been acting weird all night."

"Yeah, well, keep your worries to yourself."

"If you want to be a jerk all night," I retorted, "you can just drop me off at my house." Folding my arms over my chest, I slumped back in my seat with a huff. This was a first. Eddie had never argued with me before. My best friend was ticking me off to the point that I did not want to talk to him anymore.

By the time we had arrived at my house, there was a stony silence that you could not cut with one of those miracle knives that you see advertised on TV. Tough as diamonds! You can order this knife set toll free with three easy payments of $15.98, and still, it wouldn't have broken the tension between us.

As soon as the car came to a stop, I grabbed my purse and paintings without saying good night to Eddie. I slammed the car door behind me and stalked to the front door. For a fleeting moment, I thought that the vampire would get out and apologize. Instead, he sped out of the driveway leaving behind a cloud of dust. Heartless jerk!

I unlocked my door and stepped inside. Tears blurred my vision as I set down my artwork. I guessed I had been bottling up my feelings all during the car ride. I slumped down to the floor and cupped my head in my hands. "I try to be a good friend, and what does it get me?" I asked in between sobs. A few minutes later, I dried my wet hands on my dress. It was almost eight, and I needed someone to talk to.

Creighton answered on the third ring. "Hello?"

"Creighton, it's Shelly," I said, trying to release the enormous lump in my throat.

"Sorry I couldn't make it to your art show. I had to work overtime at the ER—Shelly, are you all right?"

"Not really. Eddie and I had a fight tonight!"

"You guys never fight! What happened?"

I relayed the events of the night to her as I got up off the floor and walked over to my stove. I put on a kettle of water. What I needed was a good cup of French vanilla cappuccino. Then Creighton finally spoke, "So, you have no idea who this person called the Chairman is?"

"No, and Eddie's silence is not helping at all. It sounds like you have an idea."

"I might. Try looking up this guy online."

"Ooh, I like that idea. Maybe he's an assassin, and Eddie has to stop him before he kills a famous politician."

"Or maybe that's the guy's code name, and he is an undercover spy."

The kettle started whistling. I shut off the stove and dumped three heaping teaspoons of cappuccino mix into a tall cup with some faded but bizarre headless cartoon characters dancing all over it. I'll never have Robin go yard sale hunting with me again. "Whatever's going on with Eddie, I'm going to get to the bottom of it."

"You go, girlfriend." Suddenly, I heard a yell in the background. "Annika, don't hit your brother!" Creighton scolded on the other end of the phone. "I'm sorry, Shelly. I'm babysitting my niece and nephew. I'll let you go. Keep me posted. Bye."

I laughed, saying good-bye. I hung up to allow Creighton to intervene on a possible fratricide. I took a sip of my fake coffee as I sat at my desk to turn on my computer. My friend's advice had rejuvenated my spirits. I turned on the computer, ready to find out why Eddie was so nervous and rude.

Two hours later, I hit my head on my desk. I hate keyword searching. When you use a common keyword like "chairman," you come up with approximately three billion hits, and that's just

the first twenty pages. After looking at the websites of the AA

chairman's minutes for last year's meeting, why Carmen Big

Wolf is Zephyr's newest chairman of the local werewolf pack,

and a video of a man break dancing on a chair, I decided that I

needed to try a different approach. My bed was looking more

and more comfortable. I shut down my computer.

As I changed into my pajamas, I thought about the day I

met Eddie. I had been a little nervous about a vampire serving

me a strawberry-banana smoothie, but once I had got to talking

with him that evening, I really started to like him. He had shown

me how to not go crazy with my telepathy by concentrating on a

few minds at a time.

"Maybe I should call him," I mused out loud, "At least, to

apologize." I picked up my cell phone and dialed Eddie's cell

phone. I heard his voice, and my heart jumped a bit with

anticipation but was met with disappointment when I realized it

was his answering machine. "Eddie, it's Shelly. I want to

apologize for tonight. I was pretty rude to you. It's just that I'm

really worried about you. I think that you're in some kind of trouble, and I just wanted to help. I mean, I still want to help. If you want to talk, call me." I hung up reluctantly. As I lay my head on the pillow, I tried to think about how I could help the vampire without getting him mad at me again.

Chapter 3:

My House Becomes a Scene from CSI

I had to work from eleven to eight the next evening. As Cricket and I walked to the library's parking lot, I saw that I had a message on my cell phone. "Maybe, it's Eddie!" Cricket suggested. I had told the fairy about our little spat last night.

"I hope so," I said. "I've been worried about him all day." My anger at the vampire had subsided the night before.

I checked my voicemail and was stunned to hear my dad say, "Shelly, it's Dad. I'm sorry to bother you at work, but have you seen Eddie? He hasn't shown up yet. Give me a call at the diner when you can."

Cricket and I looked at each other in surprise. Eddie had never shown up late for work. He is a hard worker, and wouldn't dream of taking his anger out on my father by not showing up for work. "That's really weird," I said with concern as I mounted my chocolate winged horse, Jordan, and waved good-bye to Cricket. With a beat of her beautiful wings, we flew off.

As I approached my house, I knew something was wrong. For one thing, Eddie's sleek carrot-shaped racecar was sitting in my driveway. I got off Jordan and let her graze in my overgrown lawn. She was a good horse and would not fly away.

I peered into the car window, but the only thing I saw was the keys dangling in the ignition. I shook off my concerns. Eddie had probably let himself inside with the spare key I keep under the doormat, but then again, he would never leave his car keys in plain sight. As I tried to open my door, I noticed that the security light never came on. That was strange. I never turn off my security light. I lifted up the mat. The key was still there. If Eddie were inside, how did he get in without a key?

I unlocked the front door and practically rolled into the kitchen. Eat your heart out, Jackie Chan. I reached up and felt around for the light switch. Suddenly, the room was bathed in light. Now, I am not Martha Stewart by any means, but someone or something had been in my house. Papers were all over the floor, and so was my trash. My silverware drawer was pulled out halfway, and silverware was scattered all over the room. I picked up a steak knife off a pile of papers. Suddenly, I heard a groan coming from the dark living room. I shut my eyes to see if I could read the intruder's mind. Eddie? Standing at the doorway of the living room because I didn't know if there was some else in there as well, I began to telecommunicate with him. Are you all right? Instead of an answer, I heard another groan. My friend was hurt.

I hit the living room lights. Eddie was sprawled out on the floor with a big knot on the side of his head. A blow like that would have probably killed the average person, but not a vampire. I knelt down beside him, putting the knife down on the floor. "Eddie, are you alright? What happened?"

Eddie tried to get to his feet but only got as far as his knees. Blood was dripping from a split lip. When he lifted up his head, a huge bruise covered his left eye. "Where are your paintings?" he asked me.

"My paintings? What happened here?"

"I tried to stop someone from breaking into your house."

"Who, Eddie?"

He looked at me with shame and regret as he slumped against my couch to steady himself. "I got involved with something."

"Eddie!"

"No, it's not what you think. Tony, an old friend from the bounty hunter agency that I used to work for, called me about a month ago. He's a Were who can mimic any voice. He wanted me to go undercover to help nab this sorcerer who calls himself the Chairman. This guy's selling all-natural and illegal blue mushroom fuel!" He cupped his head in his hands. "My friend was making the payments through me, but apparently he wants me to get some more solid evidence against the guy. So, he's delaying the payments."

I mentally cringed at the thought of using any colored mushroom fuel to power anything, but I concentrated on finding out what happened to my friend at my house. I put my hand on Eddie's arm. I shook my head in disbelief.

"Why didn't you tell me, or at least, my dad about it?"

"I didn't want to get anyone hurt. Tony promised me that

no one else was going to get involved. I'm such an idiot for trusting someone who screwed me over the last time we worked together!"

I could have scolded Eddie for his stupidity, but I knew that he just needed someone to talk to. "So, what happened?" I prodded.

"Well, apparently, the Chairman got wind of my late payments. That's when he sent his Treasurer."

"Is the Treasurer that elf who was there last night?"

Eddie nodded as he cupped his head in his hands. "I'm so sorry, Shelly. I had no idea that the Chairman was going to go after your paintings."

"Why would this Chairman want my paintings?"

He hesitated. "Because Tony had called the Chairman posing as me and told him that I would use your paintings to pay for my debt."

I punched the vampire hard in the arm. "You idiot," I yelled with indignation. "You know how hard I worked on those!" My best friend had gotten my paintings stolen by a mob boss. Hot tears began blurring my vision as I realized what Eddie had done to me. "I can't believe that you would do something like this!"

"You think that I wanted this, Shelly? I had no idea that Tony would use your paintings as money for his debt."

I struggled to fight back the tears. "How did your friend know where I would be?"

Eddie leaned his head. "Because I was an idiot and told Tony that you were having your paintings evaluated at the art gallery. That's why I wanted to know how much you were going to sell them for. If they were a low price, I was going to tell Tony that it wasn't worth the money. When you told me that you're weren't selling them, I asked Tony to call the whole thing off. The Chairman threatened to hurt you, and I told him I didn't want you involved anyway." Eddie knew how much I was hurting right at the moment. He reached over and gave me a hug. "I'm so sorry, Shelly. I didn't mean for any of this to happen. I had no idea that this was going to get out of hand." He looked directly into my eyes with honest regret for what he had done and strong determination to fix it. "Shelly, I'm going to make this up to you, I promise."

I almost melted when I looked into his eyes. Eddie had

that effect on me, and I knew that he was determined to get back my paintings. "So, what happened to my house?" I asked as I wiped away the tears.

"I had trouble sleeping today. So after the sun had set, I called the Chairman and told him that I wanted out of it. Not that Tony was going to bail me out. But the Chairman told me that he would get the money from me in some way. From the conversation with the Treasurer, I thought that he was going to come after you. By the time I got here, I saw this werewolf walk into your house. I thought you were home, and I didn't want you to get hurt because of my stupidity. So, I turned myself into mist and came in through a crack in the door."

"Wait a minute!" I interrupted. "How did this guy break-in?"

Eddie paused. "This guy can walk through walls!" He ran his tongue over his cut lip and winced in pain. "I tried to stop him from stealing your paintings."

I let that sink in for a moment. Eddie really cared about my paintings and me. He had taken quite a beating for trying to rescue some pictures. Finally, I spoke, "I guess I should call the police. You're going to be okay?" I asked, helping him to his feet.

Eddie nodded. Vampires heal quickly, so the knot on his head had already gone down quite a bit. "I think the paintings are the only things that are missing," he said with a sad smile. "I'm going to make this up to you. Somehow."

There is nothing quite like having your home turned into a crime scene. The boys in blue were tromping all over my kitchen floor. Several flashes from cameras flickered inside the house while Eddie and I stood outside, talking with a burly minotaur in street clothes. The name on his badge read Angus. "So, Mr. Van Helsing followed the intruder inside your home, Miss Anderson?" the creature with the head of a bull, the torso and arms of a man, and two cow-like legs asked me in a low, unmistakable gravelly voice.

I nodded as I folded my arms over my chest. The night temperature was dropping, and I was freezing to death. Eddie and I had agreed to tell the police that some random person had broken into my house and grabbed my paintings, thinking that they were worth something. With my dad as a retired police officer and Robin on the force as well, I try not to lie to the police, but something about the minotaur didn't jive with me. It sounded like the Chairman had friends in high places, and I did not want Eddie to get in any more trouble. "How long are you guys going to be here?" I asked.

"You won't be staying here tonight. I can tell you that," Detective Angus replied as if he did not care if I slept on a park bench.

He asked me some more of the standard questions and left us to continue overseeing the investigation. I accepted Eddie's offer to sleep at his place. After I went inside (with Detective Angus' permission, of course), I quickly put together an overnight bag and grabbed a light jacket. Then I made my way past all the police officers, trying not to destroy any evidence. By the time I had stepped outside, Eddie was talking on his cell phone. He saw me and pointed to the phone. "Your dad wants to talk to you," he said by the time I walked over to him.

I took the phone from the vampire. "Dad, I'm fine. Don't worry," I said, reassuring my panicking father. Dad wasn't one to normally freak out, but when a crime is committed against either

Robin or me, he has a habit of going into an

overprotective-father drive. "Someone broke into my house and

stole my paintings. Yes, I got your message. Eddie? He's all

right. He saw the guy and went in after him." I glanced

admiringly at the vampire but turned my head away so he would

not see me gawking at him. "Did Eddie tell you what happened?

He was knocked unconscious. That's why he never showed up.

If you need me, I'll be at Eddie and Dirk's. Love you, Dad." I

hung up and handed it back to Eddie.

"In case you're wondering, your dad didn't fire me," he

said with a fanged smile. He grabbed my backpack and tossed it

over his shoulder. We walked to his car, and once we got in, he

started up the engine. "You can sleep in the guest room. I

should call Dirk and let him know that we have a guest."

"Dirk working tonight?" I asked about Eddie's brother.

Dirk is a night (go figure) disc jockey at the local oldies station.

You would think that vampires like all that head-banging music,

but not Dirk. He is more of a Beatles fan. He actually looks like

an eighties rocker with his shoulder-length hair. Like his brother,

Dirk is a vegetarian. I really like hanging out with the Van Helsing brothers. Dirk has so many conspiracy theories he found while surfing on some of his favorite websites, and Eddie always trying to disprove them. It's great watching the brothers have at it.

"No, tonight's his night off."

"Does Dirk know about your problems?" I asked Eddie as we drove to his house.

Eddie shook his head. "I don't want to get him involved, either," he replied. I had no need to read his mind. I knew my friend was telling the truth.

I'm always amazed whenever I see the Van Helsing mansion. It's not a creepy mansion that you see in those cheesy horror movies. In fact, the grass green three-story house with white trim is well-kept both on the inside and out. The coolest thing about their home is the windows. They are vampire safe via UV protected panes. They block out all forms of sunlight while Eddie and Dirk can still look out of them. I had been there on several occasions, but this was going to be my first time overnight.

Eddie hit the garage door opener, and up went one of the doors. In fact, the garage looks more like an airplane hanger with his eight cars, minus the carrot car, and his two motorcycles. The vampire eased the car next to his picklemobile, and we got out.

I saw Dirk's rainbow-colored dragon sleeping in a small corner of the garage/airplane hanger. Ringo is small for a dragon as most dragons are about the size of a double-decker bus. In fact, he's not much bigger than my winged horse. We tiptoed around him. It is best to let sleeping dragons lie, especially a mean one like Ringo.

Once we got inside, Eddie offered to make me a cup of cappuccino, but knowing that I would be up all night with the caffeine in my system, I opted for a cup of hot cocoa. I sat up at the counter. "So, Eddie," I asked, "does this Chairman have a real name?"

Eddie thought for a moment. "Yeah," he said, a bit leery, "a sorcerer by the name of Mario Stregone." For some unknown reason, my friend couldn't stand sorcerers or witches. I think it might have something to do with the time he became a vampire.

"Eddie, how do you know Mario Stregone?" Dirk came into the kitchen carrying his Tombstone laptop computer. He set it on the green countertop, and that's when he noticed me sipping my hot chocolate. He looked at Eddie, then at me, and then back at Eddie. "Why is Shelly here at ten o'clock at night?" he asked us.

Eddie and I began to take turns telling him what had happened this evening. Then with a little mental shove from me, that was something to the effect of tell Dirk everything, or I'll stab you with a wooden stake, Eddie told him what he had been doing for the past month.

"Eddie, you moron!" Dirk exclaimed when his brother had finished. "You know who Mario Stregone is? He's the head of a mob gang called the Board of Directors!"

"I can't believe you even set Shelly up!"

"Oh, we've already had this discussion, Dirk."

Eddie held out his hands. "I never meant for any of this to get out of hand. And for your information, I never set Shelly up."

"Oh right," Dirk said, "Stregone's just a good citizen trying to help out. Come on, I hope you're not that naïve. He was selling you illegal mushroom fuel! Didn't that raise any red

flags?"

"Look," Eddie said in a pathetic effort to defend himself, "I

trusted Tony. He was the one who left me high and dry."

"That's not the point," Dirk retorted. "You got yourself

wrapped up in the mob."

Eddie scowled at his brother. I knew what he was

thinking. He couldn't stand it if Dirk were right. So, I decided to

come up with a neutral solution. "Why don't we go down to the

police and ask Robin about this mob boss?"

"Okay, we will. Just as long as you don't mention why

we're asking," Eddie made me promise.

"Deal!"

Two vampires and a human walk into a police station. I

know that sounds like the beginning of a bad joke, but that's

what I felt like when we approached the front desk where an elf

was twirling around his swivel chair. He stopped abruptly when

Eddie gave a needless cough. The dispatcher's face turned

bright red. "How may I help you?" he said loud and professional enough to make sure that he wouldn't get into any trouble if his superiors were listening.

"Is Officer Robin Anderson around?" I asked him, suppressing a mocking laugh. "I'm his sister."

"Well, I haven't seen him, but let me call him on his walkie-talkie. He might be in the building." He picked up a gargantuan, navy blue two-way radio. In fact, it reminded me of the first cell phones. "Officer Anderson, we need you to 10-19 for a 10-42 and S-13, 10-64?"

"Kurt?" my brother's voice crackled over the radio. A long pause. I knew Robin was trying to figure out what ten codes the dispatcher was using. "I'm in the break room, and I have no idea what you just said."

Kurt's voice faltered. "Well, officer, your sister is here with two vampires," he said. He looked ready to move if Eddie or Dirk tried to bite him (which they wouldn't'.)

"Oh," Robin replied, unaffected by the news. "Tell them I'm coming up. Over and out." I could only imagine my brother breaking out into laughter.

It only took a few seconds for my brother to walk into the

lobby. "Hey, Shelly!" he said to me. "Hi, Dirk. Hi, Eddie." As

soon as he acknowledged their presence, he turned his attention

to me. "Shelly, I heard about the break-in. Are you okay?" he

asked me in his big-brother-taking-care-of his-little-sister voice.

We're only a year apart

I nodded. "The only things that got stolen were my

paintings. I wasn't home when it happened."

He looked at Eddie. "And I heard that you tried to save

the day!" He pretended to jab the vampire in the gut. "You sly

dog!" Robin always teases me about having a crush on Eddie,

which I have always vehemently denied.

I ignored my brother. "Does Detective Angus have any

leads on my case?" I asked.

Robin shook his head. "Nah, and if he does, he wouldn't

tell me about it. So, what's the real reason you guys came down

here at this hour?" he asked us.

"Actually," Dirk began, "I'm doing some research on

famous mob bosses here in Zephyr, and I was wondering if you

guys would know anything about Mario Stregone. It's for my

radio show." On the way to the police station, Eddie and I had volunteered Dirk to ask the questions.

"Oh, every officer knows about Stregone," Robin said. "He's the head of a gang called the Board of Directors. Calls himself the Chairman."

Dirk and I both rolled our eyes at Eddie, but Robin never caught on. "Interesting," Dirk commented as he pretended to jot down the information on a crumpled piece of paper that he had pulled out of his pocket. He was really writing his name over and over again, but my brother couldn't tell the difference. "Why haven't you caught him yet?"

"Unfortunately, we don't have anything concrete to book him on."

This Stregone was a regular Al Capone. He could get away with murder. I wondered if he had any problems with tax evasion. Then I had a brilliant question. "Off the record, Robin," I asked in a low voice, "is Stregone bribing any of the officers here?"

Robin pulled me aside and whispered in my ear. "I'm helping out with an internal investigation. Some of the case files on Stregone have disappeared within the last few months. That's all I can tell you."

"Oh," I said. Detective Angus was probably taking bribes

from Stregone, and that's why he didn't have any leads on the

break-in. Of course, I could be wrong and paranoid. I glanced at

my watch. It was almost midnight, and my brain was slowly

running on vapors. "I guess we better get going. Thanks, Robin.

You're the best." I gave him a big hug, which surprised him. "I'm

staying with these guys, just so you know."

"I'll let you know if Detective Angus has any leads. See

you guys later!" Robin waved good-bye to us as we left the

station.

Eddie showed me to my room. It was so huge it might

have been a third master bedroom. I nearly fell into the pile of

six plush purple pillows (try saying that ten times fast) on the

king-sized bed. A huge eight-drawer, cherry dresser, topped with

a fancy iron rod mirror, was across from the purple bed. "This is

nice!" I said aloud to no one in particular because Eddie and Dirk

had already left me alone. An interesting thing about my

telepathy is that I can't read the thoughts of the undead if they aren't in the same room as me. This is a good thing sometimes.

Especially considering my mixed feelings, I was starting to have

towards Eddie.

With my pajamas slung over my shoulder, I wandered into

the adjoining bathroom and tossed the two-gallon Zippy Lock

bag that contained my toothbrush, toothpaste, travel shampoo

and conditioner, and crucial hair supplies on the counter. I

changed and crawled into bed. I tried to think about everything

that had happened this evening, but my thoughts were running

together like oatmeal. I finally drifted off to la-la land.

La-la land turned into a dark nightmare as shadows

crossed paths into my dreams. I was standing at the beginning of

my driveway. I saw figures enter my house and carry away my

belongings. "No! No!" I screamed.

I sat up in bed. It took me a moment to realize that I was

sleeping at Eddie's house. No one was creeping into my house

to steal what little valuables I had. It was just a dream.

I heard someone knocking on the bedroom door. "Shelly,

are you okay?" Eddie asked through the door.

I got up out of bed and opened the door. Eddie was

standing in the doorway. "Yeah, I'm fine. I just had a bad dream."

"I'm so sorry about all of this." He sighed. "Maybe, I'm just a sucker for helping a friend out."

I put a hand on his arm. "Well, this friend isn't going to leave you high and dry. Thanks for checking up on me."

After Eddie left, I lay back against my pillow. I thought I lived in a safe neighborhood, but now I wasn't so sure. "Maybe, I'm just paranoid," I told myself. "It was just a one-time thing. The Chairman got my paintings." What was I so worried about? At least, Eddie was kind enough to let me crash at his place, and I felt really safe in his house. It took me a while, but I finally drifted back to a dreamless sleep.

Chapter 4:

I Get to Read the Mind of a Drug Addict

Eddie and Dirk were already asleep when I left for work
the next morning. Contrary to public belief, vampires don't sleep
in coffins during the day. They sleep in regular beds, just like the
rest of the world. Dirk would go crazy if he ever slept in a coffin.
He is very claustrophobic. That's why he will never ride in one of
Eddie's cars.

I pawed through the kitchen, looking for something to eat.
I finally found the last bagel and spread some peanut butter on
it. I was too lazy to heat up the bagel. I spent the next ten
minutes hunting for a piece of paper and something to write with.
With twenty drawers in the kitchen, you would think that I would
find something else other than a pink napkin and a red crayon.
Nothing like reading red on pink if you like going blind at an early
age. I wrote a thank you note to the guys, telling them I would let

them know if I needed their services. I was tempted to put a little heart on the note next to Eddie's name, but I thought better of it. What was going on with me? Was I falling for the vampire? I shook my head to get out of it. Then I headed off to work on Jordan. I had sent her to the Van Helsing's last night when Eddie and I had left my house.

On my morning break, I was sitting on the ugly, but quite comfy pink leather couch reading the Zephyr Herald. Other than the front page, the editorials, and the comics, I rarely read any other part of the paper, so I had no idea why I suddenly felt the urge to peruse the socialite section. Actually, it's more like a couple of columns instead of an entire article. That's when my eyes caught something very interesting. This Thursday evening at six o'clock, the richest man in Zephyr, Mario Stregone, was holding an exclusive dinner party at his home in Rockfort Hills. I had to show Eddie this. I made a photocopy of the article and tucked it into my pants pocket.

As soon as I walked up to the front desk, Raquel handed me the phone. "Shelly," she said, "you got a phone call."

Nodding my thanks, I took the phone from her. "Hello, this is Shelly," I said.

"Miss Anderson? This is Detective Angus."

"Oh!" I said, hoping for some good news about the break-in.

"I want you to come down to the station to file charges."

"Why?"

"We caught the Were who broke into your house."

I was surprised. He was a fast-moving cop, or something wasn't just right about the whole thing. "That was fast! When is a good time for me to come down?"

"Five-thirty?"

"Sounds good. I'll be there. Thank you, Detective Angus." After I hung up the phone, I was puzzled. I tried to remember what Eddie and I told the police about the break-in. Eddie did say that a werewolf had broken in, but he never mentioned to Detective Angus how the guy broke in. Anyway, the description he gave both me and the police was pretty sketchy. Well, I would find out down at the station.

I got off Jordan and tied her to a post in the visitor parking space outside the Zephyr Police Department. How many times had I gone through these doors in the last twenty-four hours? Too many times, I dare say. I checked my watch. Once again, I was fifteen minutes early. Kurt, the dispatcher, was apparently off that evening, and I was greeted by a more mature eighteen-year-old satyr. "I'm here to see Detective Angus."

He jerked his thumb to his left. "Last door on your right."

"Thanks," I read the name badge that was pinned to his blue shirt, "Mathias." I walked down the long-range of open and closed doors. It was a long eerie hallway, and I thought that I was hearing voices for a moment. There are three undead people in the employment of the Zephyr police department, a ghost and two werewolves, and they were not around that I could tell. I stopped dead in my tracks once I heard someone say the name, Stregone. I gave a silent gasp as I realized who was talking. Detective Angus was in his office, talking on his phone.

I try not to eavesdrop on people's conversations. I have enough problems already with being a telepath. But the minotaur's phone conversation compelled me to listen in. "Don't worry about it, Mr. Stregone. Everything has been taken care of." I heard the minotaur say. I knew that Detective Angus was indeed a lousy cop. I gave a quick knock on the doorframe. I smiled as I suddenly heard the phone hit the cradle really hard. Busted! "Detective Angus?" I asked innocently. "It's Shelly Anderson."

"Oh, come on in!" he told me nonchalantly.

I opened the door and stepped inside the stuffy office. Everything felt fake to me. The expensive oak desk looked out of place and was very pretentious-looking in the tiny room with cheap striped wallpaper. Even when Dad was a police detective, his paycheck would've never been able to cover the cost of the desk. I wondered how much the Chairman paid for Angus' brand-new coal-black Italian suit. It was like the minotaur was putting on a show. Give 'em the old razzle-dazzle. "I know I'm a bit early. You said that you arrested the man who broke into my house," I said to him.

"I did," the bull-man said as he reached into an opened drawer and pulled out a file. He showed me a picture of an old werefox, both in his human and fox form. "Do you recognize him?"

I shook my head. "I wasn't the one who saw the intruder. It was Eddie."

Detective Angus just nodded. "This is Oozie Vixen, a small-time kleptomaniac and junkie. When he becomes a werefox, he can change into a movable puddle of ooze. He has quite the record with us."

I didn't buy his story. "Are you sure?" I asked, "because Eddie said it was a werewolf, not a werefox."

Detective Angus shrugged. "Werewolf, werefox. They're all the same to me."

Suddenly, a light bulb clicked on in the darkness of my mind. "Can I see the guy who broke into my house?" I asked. "Maybe, I know him from the library."

"Sure, he's down in the holding station. I'll take you down there." Detective Angus said as he got up from his plush leather chair. I followed him down the hall, and then we made a sharp right. We walked into a large room where there were six tiny rooms, each surrounded with thick iron bars. In the last cell, I saw him. Oozie Vixen was curled up in the fetal position, rocking back and forth on his cot. He was going through withdrawal. I knew it was the wrong man because there was no bruising on his face. Were folk don't heal as quickly as vampires do. Eddie had put up a good fight, and this guy was so out of his mind that he couldn't even fight off a baby. I seriously began to doubt if I could read his mind. I was wondering how the police were holding a werefox who could literally slip through anything when the guard sitting at a nearby desk spoke up. "Most of these cells are magic inhibiting. When we hold a slippery prisoner who possesses magical abilities, we throw him into one," he explained in an answer to the puzzled look on my face.

I looked at the older Welkie. For those who don't know, the Welkie is a unique form of the human race. Any Welkie can live for centuries, have all types of magic, and are trained to become wizards and enchantresses. "So, you must be the wizard who built that cell."

The guard nodded. "Sergeant Lionel Copperfield." He introduced himself as he shook my hand. "Detective Angus said that's the guy who broke into your house," he said, pointing to the spaced-out werefox. "Do you recognize him?"

"I have to get a closer look at him. Can I?" Copperfield nodded, and I stepped closer to the cell. Only family and close friends know that I can read the minds of the undead, and so the Welkie and the minotaur had no idea what I was doing. I concentrated on the Were's mind patterns.

I need a fix now. Didn't do it, didn't do it. I need some smack now. No lawyer. Lies, liar. Paintings can't buy drugs. Need a fix. Bright circles dancing all around me. Make them stop! Need it, need it, need it. Don't know of any paintings. I'm hungry. Why don't they believe me? I didn't rob anyone.

I shook myself from the stoned guy's mind. If I tried to read it anymore, I would have to commit myself into a white padded room. "It's probably him," I lied to Detective Angus and Sergeant Copperfield. "Thank you for letting me see him, but I don't think I'll press charges."

Angus looked at me skeptically. "Really?"

I racked my brain for a believable answer. "Uh, um," I stammered, "I—He looks like he doesn't need to go to jail. He just needs counseling."

"Well, we won't charge him with breaking and entering,

but we did find him in possession of illegal drugs," the minotaur replied.

"Oh!" I remembered something that I wanted to ask him. "When can I return home?"

"Anytime you want. We've collected all the evidence that we need," he replied as he led me back to the station lobby.

Right! Crime scenes don't clean up that fast, whether you're in a magical land or not. I thanked him for his "helpfulness" and hurried out the door. Once I was outside, I breathed a huge sigh of relief. I wasn't planning on going to the diner tonight, but I needed to tell Eddie the new development.

Chapter 5:

Eddie is Threatened with Blackmail

It was already sunset when I arrived at Anderson's Place. The diner is a cross between a Denny's and a sports bar. The inside is bright and well lit with its pale yellow walls. Each one of the ten black square tables can seat four people and has a clear plastic covering over the colored tablecloths that make for an easy clean-up. Near the ice cream bar where Eddie works is a pool table, courtesy of the Count and Countess Von Stoker. Every Friday is Billiards Night when Robin, Strider, Dirk, and even Eddie play several rounds of pool. Dad had turned the old building into a family restaurant.

It was reasonably busy for a Wednesday night. Eddie was busy serving soda and ice cream drinks at the counter located back in the diner when I waved to get his attention. "Eddie, Eddie!" I almost shouted.

The vampire shot an annoyed look at me. I knew that

look. Eddie hates it when I interrupt him while he's serving

customers. I hopped up on my usual green leather stool and

watched Eddie serve a satyr and a nymph, their root beer floats.

Because my mom was killed by a drunk driver, my dad doesn't

serve any kind of alcohol at his diner. I'm not saying that my dad

is a snobby teetotaler. He doesn't drink but doesn't mind other

people having a few beers as long as it's not too excessive. But

Dad doesn't encourage drinking and driving (or flying or riding),

and pretty much none of his customers complain about his

no-alcohol policy.   I waited until the vampire was done, and then

I snapped my fingers. "Hey, Eddie, I'll have a cream soda!" I

said.

Eddie came over to me. "What are you doing, Shelly?" he

asked.

"I want a cream soda," I said, trying to hide my smile.

Eddie's dashing eyes brightened. "With a dash of

strawberry?"

"Oh, of course," I said. I watched as the vampire turned

his back to me and began to pour cream soda into a tall glass.

Eddie looked really cute in his royal blue short-sleeve, buttoned shirt, and black jeans. I surprised myself with that observation. Where did that come from? Back to reality, Shelly.

"What are you thinking about, Shelly?" Eddie had set the glass on the countertop and was now looking at me.

"Nothing," I lied, other than the fact that you look really cute tonight. I sipped my strawberry cream soda thoughtfully. "This is good, Eddie. Thanks."

"You're welcome," Eddie replied as he gave me his unforgettable fanged smile. "Okay, either you have a really boring social life, or you have something urgent to tell me."

I glanced around, making sure that nobody was acting suspiciously around me. I leaned forward and whispered, "I spoke with Detective Angus earlier. He said that he caught the robber."

"Why are you whispering?"

I was about to tell him why when we both heard my dad shout from the kitchen, "Eddie, can you wait on tables 9, 2, and 7?"

"Sure, Mr. Anderson!" the vampire called back. He checked his watch. "Look, I go on break in about a half-hour.

Mind covering the counter for me for a few minutes?"

"Uh, sure." I got off my seat and walked around to the back of the counter. I was used to serving customers here. In fact, before I became a librarian, I used to work here. I served the satyr and the nymph another round of root beer floats when my favorite werecat came into the diner. Gemini Sher Khan walked up to the counter. "Hi," I said cheerfully. "What can I get for you?"

"Two double scoops of chocolate ice cream for me, please, Shelly," Gemini replied. When she is in her cat form, Gemini is a beautiful orange tiger, and tonight she looked lovely in her green three-quarter sleeve shirt and dark brown jeans. Gemini is the only Were person I know who hates her superpower. She always tells me, "The only time I'm actually able to duplicate myself is when I am cooking two things at the same time. I mean, if I doubled myself all the time, it would freak people out."

"Where's Tucker?'" I asked her. Gemini was seldom without her boyfriend, another werecat by the name of Tucker Tigris.

"Oh, he had to work overtime at the butcher shop. He was freezing the leftover meat when I spoke to him last." Tucker has the power to freeze things. "Where's Eddie?" Gemini asked, finally realizing that the vampire was not at the counter.

"Waiting on tables," I replied as I pointed to where Eddie was balancing a tray full of food. "He asked me to cover for him." I began to fill up a waffle cone with chocolate ice cream for Gemini.

"Are you all right?" Gemini asked. "I heard about the break-in."

"Oh, I'm fine."

Eddie came back behind the counter. He was done waiting on tables, for now. "Hey, Gemini! What are you talking about?" he asked us.

"Gemini wanted to know about the break-in," I replied. By the time I was done relaying the story for the millionth time, I had asked Gemini how her day was at Wisteria's Catering.

"Oh, it went great. We weren't asked to cater to Mario Stregone's business party."

I noticed Eddie tense up at the mention of the Chairman's

name. The vampire's thoughts told me that he was still anxious about the Chairman hurting, or even worse, killing me. The sorcerer obviously knew where I lived and worked, and Eddie knew that I might be in danger. I held back a sudden blush. "Why, Gemini?" I asked.

"Mr. Stregone, the great philanthropist that he is," Gemini said with a roll of her green cat eyes, "wouldn't even pay his bill in full the last time we catered one of his great revelries. Wisteria, my boss, was so ticked off at him that she almost threw a fiesta herself."

"I've heard little about Stregone's parties," I lied. I just learned about the existence of the sorcerer only last night. Suddenly, I had an idea of how to get Eddie out of his debt and get back my paintings. "What are Stregone's parties like?" I asked the weretiger as I handed the ice cream cone to her.

"Oh," she said as she handed me some money for her purchase, "everyone dresses up in designer clothes that none of us can buy even with our salaries combined. You would not believe the security at his parties. It's like he's a high-profile politician or a crime boss."

Eddie and I glanced at each other. How right she was, and she didn't even know it! "Sounds like an exclusive party," the vampire replied as he opened the cash register and handed Gemini her change.

"Tell me about it!" Gemini said. Then her cell phone rang, and she picked it up. "Hey, baby," she said as she walked away from us, chatting away with Tucker.

"I can see why you wanted to help me out."

Eddie and I both looked up to see a werewolf in his mid-thirties sitting at the end of the counter. He was wearing camouflage cargo pants and a pair of military-grade boots and a black leather jacket over a black T-shirt. The other customers who were sitting at the bar quickly left after the Were shot them a warning glare.

Eddie came over to the werewolf, but refused to shake his hand and didn't even crack a smile. Instead, he folded his arms across his chest. "It's better than getting shot at, Tony."

Tony took 500 druci out of his wallet and handed it to the vampire. "I'm leaving town in about an hour, and I just wanted to pay you for your help."

Eddie shook his head. "I don't want your dirty money. All I want is the reason why you had to involve my friend."

Tony glanced over at me before answering. He realized who the vampire was talking about. "That's your friend? Look, Eddie, you know the business. People get caught in the crossfire."

"Only if you shove them in the line of fire!" Eddie snapped at him. He slammed his hands on the top of the counter, which made me jump with surprise and glared at his former friend.

Tony laughed. "Still caring for the little people, Eddie?"

"Don't say that about Shelly!"

"You have a thing for her, don't you?"

Eddie glanced over at me, realizing that I was waiting for both verbal and mental reply and carefully answered, "That's not the point! You promised to get nobody else involved. You set her up. One of Stregone's men broke into her house. She could've been hurt or even killed."

Tony shrugged carelessly. "Things happen!"

Eddie's jaw dropped as did mine. The selfish little prick was only in it for his client's money and could care less about what happened to us. As I continued to read the Were's mind, I learned that he was going to skip town and leave Eddie to clean up his mess. The truth was that Tony didn't want to deal with the Chairman anymore.

I immediately sent Eddie a telepathic message about Tony's plans.

Eddie nodded at me and decided to play it cool. "So, why are you leaving, Tony?"

He shrugged. "I'm a P.I., now, Eddie. You know that. I've got bigger fish to fry."

I was very impressed that my friend was doing a great job keeping his rising temper under control. "You've got enough evidence to put him away," he hissed.

"He's not on the top of my list anymore. A client hired me for a case with a lot more money involved. Sorry, Eddie, but there's nothing I can do."

"You can do the right thing!"

Tony chuckled. "Still the same old Eddie? Always trying to be the hero. I didn't get into the bounty hunter business and private investigations to help people."

What a loser! This guy only looked out for himself. I waited for Eddie's response.

"Get out!" Eddie growled at Tony. "Don't ever contact me again!"

Tony sat back in shock. He didn't expect Eddie to cut him out of his life. Without saying another word, he got up and left the dinner. Once the werewolf was gone, I looked over at the vampire. "With friends like that, who needs enemies," I said dryly. "You okay?"

"I've been better," he replied. He ran his fingers through his curly black hair. "I should have known that he would do this."

After a short silence, Eddie checked his watch, still fuming over his friend's betrayal. As if my dad timed it perfectly, he allowed Eddie to go on break. I grabbed the vampire's hand and led him over to an empty booth far away from the crowd. A centaur that I didn't recognize tended the counter.

"Shelly, what are you doing?" Eddie asked me the second we sat down.

"New guy?" I asked, referring to the centaur.

Eddie grunted in response, irritated at the fact that I had

pulled him over here to ask about the waiter. "Tanner Centauro. Your dad hired him last week. Now, answer my question."

I told him about my encounter with Detective Angus. He listened intently as I told him about the tripped-out werefox. "And before you say anything—yes, I did read the guy's mind."

"How was that?" Eddie asked.

I shuddered, recalling the experience. "I never want to reread a junkie's mind. It was awful. It was like trying to put three jigsaw puzzles together at the same time."

"You hate jigsaw puzzles."

"Exactly. I really think Stregone paid Angus to arrest Vixen so that the werewolf who broke into my house could get off scot-free." Then I remembered the article. I reached into my pants pocket and showed Eddie the paper. "Read this. It says that Stregone is hosting a private party on Thursday evening at six o'clock in his home in Rockfort Hills."

"Thank you for letting me read the article," Eddie replied sarcastically.

"Pay attention!" I said. "Look, I had this great idea. We dress up, go in, grab my paintings, and get out. It's that simple."

As I told him my plan, the vampire's eyes widened in horror. He couldn't believe what I was proposing to do. "Have you lost your so-called mind?" he asked me.

"How hard can it be? We get in, grab my paintings, and get out."

Eddie shook his head sadly. "You obviously have never crashed a party before," he said. "Shelly, this is a dangerous and dumb idea. I'm not going to crash a mob boss's party when he is holding six hundred druci over my head!"

I folded my arms over my chest. "Then, I'll just mention to Dad about you consorting with the mob."

Eddie's jaw dropped. "You wouldn't!"

I merely nodded. "Try me!"

"That's blackmail!"

I looked Eddie squarely in the eye. "You got me involved with Stregone, and now he has my paintings. We are doing this, understand?" I demanded. "And besides, Tony's not going to help us. We're on our own."

Eddie gave a defeated sigh. I was, of course, right all along. "What's your plan?" he asked reluctantly.

"When do you get out of work?" I answered, once again, not answering his question.

"Eleven-thirty."

I rubbed my hands together. "Good," I said enthusiastically. "Meet me at my place at midnight. And bring some cash!" I got up to leave, but Eddie grabbed my arm.

"What are you doing?" he asked me.

"I'm going to go home and get some sleep. See you at twelve." I waved good-bye and headed out the door. I got home, ate a ham and cheese Hot Pocket for dinner, and then went to bed.

My alarm clock went off at eleven-thirty. Rubbing my eyes, I crawled out of bed. I changed into a pink ribbed short sleeve shirt and a pair of blue jeans. I found my favorite pair of black sandals under the bed. I remember the first time I wore them. Eddie had told me that they were cute on me. "I'm definitely wearing this tonight," I said as I slipped my feet into them. Then I heard knocking on my door. I grabbed my purse and unlocked the door for Eddie.

The vampire was holding his motorcycle helmet under his arm. He was wearing the jean jacket I had gotten him for Christmas last year, and he looked hot in it. Then he handed me the overnight bag that I had left at his house. "You forgot this!"

I placed the bag on the kitchen table. Then I locked up my house. "Thanks for dropping it off."

"No problem! Hope you don't mind riding my motorcycle tonight?" he asked me.

"No, not at all," I replied. We walked to Eddie's red motorcycle with the little plastic box behind the back seat. It was going to be useful for our little excursion. When I was little, one of my dad's friends had a motorcycle, but my mom would not let Robin or I ride it for fear of an accident. Of course, if my mom had known that Eddie was a safe driver whenever I rode with him, she might have reconsidered. I climbed on the back of the motorcycle and put on the extra helmet that Eddie always kept around.

The vampire started up the engine. "Where are we going?" he asked.

"To the Moonlight Mall, the one that's open 24/7!" I yelled

over the roar of the engine. Eddie released the kickstand and turned the throttle to forward, and we sped down the roadway. I was holding onto the side rails so I wouldn't fall off when I wished that I could hold onto his waist instead. This wasn't the first time I had ridden with Eddie, so I wasn't scared of riding. What was I afraid of? Ruining the great friendship we had just so I could tell him that I was developing a crush on him!

Have you ever gotten that feeling that you were being followed? It is like the scene in the movies where the helpless damsel is wandering down a dark hallway. She starts thinking that she hears footsteps behind her, but of course, the noise stops when she does. Instead of looking for the source of the weird noises, she ignores the whole thing. Then suddenly, a man steps out from behind a pillar and shoots her down. I kind of felt like that damsel in distress halfway to the mall. It was pitch black outside, except for the three flickering street lights on Main Street. We were the only people on the road. Or so I thought. I glanced over my shoulder. Combined with the sudden crick in my neck and my horrific night vision, I couldn't see anything.

Eddie, I telecommunicated, *I think we're being followed.*

Really? By who?

I can't see. Your night vision's better than mine. Vampires can see the outlines of thermal heat and know if something is alive, undead, or just plain dead.

Eddie casually made a U-turn and pulled over to the side of the road. The vampire put his foot on the pavement while his right hand gripped the brake. I pointed to where I thought I saw something. *I don't see anything, he told me. He snorted. You're paranoid, Shelly.*

I am not.

Are too.

My response was a playful punch to the small of his back.

"Ow!" Eddie said aloud. "That hurt."

"I could've done it harder."

"Yeah, I bet." He started up the motorcycle again, and we headed toward the mall. "Still think the Bogeyman is following us?" he asked over the roar of the engine.

"Now, you're just making fun of me," I replied. I decided to let it go. It was past midnight, and I had just got up. Eddie was

probably right. I was just paranoid.

74

Chapter 6:

I Tell Some Lies and Buy a Boa

I was so lost in my own little world that I didn't even notice when the motorcycle came to a complete stop in a poorly lit parking space. We got off and walked into the two-story mall. All of the undead were out. I dragged the reluctant Eddie to a costume shop where a blond-haired vampire was picking up some fake jewelry off the floor. "Excuse me, ma'am?" I asked her.

She looked up at us quizzically. She was expecting to see two vampires, not one with a telepathic human, especially this late at night. "Can I help you with something?" she asked us, looking directly at Eddie, batting her eyes coquettishly.

I felt a twinge of jealousy but stopped myself. Who am I kidding? I wasn't dating him or anything. "Actually, we're looking for a couple of wigs," I replied.

"The last aisle on your left." The vampire turned around and went back to pick up the stuff that some inconsiderate kids had pulled off the shelf. How hard is it to put things back where you got them? I could empathize with her. I was always reshelving out-of-place books.

Once we arrived in the aisle, I began looking for a decent wig that did not look like a certified rat's nest. Eddie had his right elbow on one of the shelves and had his hand resting on the side of his head. He was bored and had no idea what I was up to.

"Sorry, Eddie," I said as I tried on a bright blue wig. "I want us to be in disguise when we go to Stregone's party." I turned around to face him. "What do you think?"

"Just add giant shoes and a big red nose, and you'll be all set," Eddie replied with a slight smirk.

"Ha, ha! No!" I tossed the wig to the vampire. "Now, you try it on," I said.

"No problem," Eddie said as he pulled the wig over his curly hair. "God, I wish I could see myself in a mirror because there's no doubt that I look good."

"Yeah, good enough to join the circus."

We both started laughing. "Ah, touché!" Eddie replied. He took off the horrific wig and pointed to a natural red-headed one. "You'd look perfect in that one, Shelly."

"What?" I asked, not really expecting Eddie to say that.

"Oh, come on, Eddie!" I said.

"No, I'm serious. Try it on,"

I pulled the beautiful red wig over my shoulder-length brown hair. It felt really nice, not itchy like the cheap ones you find at the dollar store. I ran my fingers through the delicate strands of hair. I whipped my head around the second I heard the low whistle. "Like it?" I asked Eddie.

"Yeah, you look good." Actually, what he was really thinking was that I looked really nice. Eddie's very careful about his thoughts whenever I'm with him.

I took off the wig. "Glad you approve. I'm going to buy it." I looked around the small collection of men's wigs. "Now, we need a wig for you." I picked up a fluffy black one.

"I'm not wearing a Fro!" Eddie protested. "Do you know how dorky I will look in that?"

"Now that you mention it. Come on, be a sport, and put it on."

Eddie grumbled and threw on the wig. He was right. I covered my mouth, trying to stifle a fit of hysterical laughter. "You're the Devil," Eddie said.

"Actually, I'm the Devil's sister." I reached up and pushed up the front of the wig. "There," I said in a motherly voice. "Now, I can see your eyes. Boy, do you look mad!" I grabbed the price tag. "And it's only ten bucks. It'll be perfect for the party!"

"Just to appease you, I'll pay for it myself," he reluctantly agreed as he pulled it off. He combed his hair back into place with his slender fingers. "But one condition. You never make me wear it in public again after this party. Promise?"

I nodded. Now, what else did we need? We were going to buy clothes at another store. I sprinted to the aisle with the plastic necklaces and those flashing bracelets that you find at the bottom of the treasure chest at the doctor's office. I looked around and realized that my friend was nowhere in sight. "Hey, Eddie!" I called.

The vampire suddenly came around the corner. "Yes, master?" he said. His striking green eyes held a bored look in them. "What do you want?" he asked.

"I thought we might need some accessories!"

Eddie rubbed his temples with the tips of his fingers. "Why me?" he asked aloud to no one in particular.

I spotted a long necklace with pale blue pearls. They would go well with my cocktail dress. "Do you think that these would go well with my dress?"

"Which one?" Eddie groaned.

"The one I wore to the gallery."

"Oh, yeah! That one. Sure, whatever makes you happy." He was being the typical guy, not listening. He had his back turned to me. I turned to see what was holding his interest so long. He was fingering a long gold chain necklace that was hanging off a peg hook.

"Found something you like?" I asked.

"Yeah!" He slipped the necklace over his head and undid the first three buttons of his shirt. He turned slowly around to face me. "How do I look?" he asked.

Be still, my fluttering heart! I struggled for words. Here I was staring at four inches of hunky vampire chest, and I was speechless. God, Shelly, I reprimanded myself, Eddie's your best friend, and you're staring at him like a deer in the headlights.

I guess I hadn't answered Eddie yet. "Earth to Shelly!" he

said as he waved his hand in front of my face.

I snapped back to reality and remembered my friend's question. "Yeah, you'd look great with that necklace on!" I said.

"I thought you would approve. Actually, I was thinking about wearing that red shirt with this fine piece of jewelry." The vampire took off the necklace and held it in his hand.

"Not that shirt, Eddie," I said, knowing exactly which one he was referring to. The shirt was not just red. It had bright orange polka dots about the size of Texas all over it. I had told Eddie the first time I saw him wearing that eyesore with the big, billowy sleeves, and I quote, "The next time I see you wearing that thing, I will stab you multiple times with a wooden stake, and then drag your sorry body into the blazing sun to serve as a warning to others who dare to wear shirts that went out of style thirty years ago." I have never seen Eddie wear that shirt again.

Eddie held his hands defensively. "Okay, I'll find another shirt instead," Evidently, he remembered my threat. "Are you almost done?" he asked me. "'Cause I'm starving!"

"Oh, quit your whining!" I replied.

"I'm bored out of my freaking skull here!"

"What makes you say that?" I asked, knowing perfectly well what his answer would be.

"Well," said Eddie, "I am a guy, and you are a girl. We're doing stuff only you are supposed to do."

"Okay, do you not want to crash the party?" I said.

"No! This is the worst idea you've come up with!"

"Whose paintings got stolen?

"Yours," Eddie replied. Then he sighed dramatically. "I worked through my lunch break because someone called in sick. Therefore, I'm starving! Can we please wrap this up and get something to eat?"

I shook my head and walked up to the front of the store with all our merchandise. I paid for my wig and the pearl necklace. "Going to a costume party?" the clerk asked us.

"Yeah," I said. And hoping against hope that we don't get killed there. I said nothing else as she handed me back my change. Then I waited for Eddie to pay for his necklace and his fro for what seemed like a long time. Eddie likes to write checks, and he takes his own sweet time doing it.

We walked to a sub shop in the food court. After a mental debate on who would pay for the food, I finally gave in and let Eddie be the gentleman. He ordered a Caesar salad with a bottle of grape-flavored water, and I ordered my favorite: a meatball sub with a medium-size root beer. We sat down at a table for two and began to eat when I glanced over Eddie's left shoulder to see the elf that had been pushing my friend around at the gallery. Elf at nine o'clock, I told Eddie mentally while taking a sip of my soda.

Eddie gave a discreet nod and casually glanced over his shoulder. *It's the Treasurer,* he told me subliminally.

Do you think he followed us here?

I don't know, but let's talk so that he won't suspect anything. "So, how was work?" he asked me.

I hesitated for a long time. I was trying my best not to look at the elf, so instead, I started talking to my sub. "It was good," I replied without looking up. "I had to move five rows of books today so that we could have some room on the shelves."

"Oh, that's cool. How long did it take you?"

"I don't know. A long time."

Your sandwich isn't going to be much for conversation. Look at me. Eddie pointed to himself. "It was pretty busy at the diner today. I've got the funniest story. This guy came in . . ."

I only half-heard the tale. I watched the elf out of the corner of my eye. This whole acting like it was just a normal night thing wasn't working. The guy must know we're on to him. I involuntarily grabbed Eddie's wrist. The guy's creeping me out, Eddie. I glanced around, looking for a way out.

Where's mall security when you really need it? Probably sitting in front of a bunch of security monitors eating a box of doughnuts. Then I heard the sound of four hooves coming into the food court. I breathed a huge sigh of relief when I saw the coal-black centaur. If you were to see a centaur coming at you head-on, he looks like an average human from the waist up, but the rest of him is a horse's body. I got up without warning and made my way toward the centaur wearing the black mall security guard uniform. "Excuse me, sir," I said in a low whisper.

The horse-man was well over six feet tall but had a kindly look on his sixty-something face. "Yes, miss?" he asked in a husky voice that was filled with the strong scent of cigarette smoke. He must read the anxiety on my face. "Is there something wrong?"

"Yes, that man over there," I said, pointing to Uncle Creepy. "He's my ex, and he's been violating his restraining order. I was wondering if you could get him away from my boyfriend and me. Don't bother about calling the police. Just get him away from me." Another convincing smile to go along with my little fib.

The centaur nodded. He trotted over to the elf. Out of the corner of my eye, I saw him tell the elf to get out. Our stalker made a big deal at first but backed off when the centaur reached for his stun gun. Once the elf (being personally escorted by mall security) was out of sight, I walked back to our table, smiling satisfactorily.

Eddie was shocked at my little feat. "How did you do that?" he asked.

"I told a little white lie."

He looked at me quizzically, raising his right eyebrow. "Care to indulge?" he asked.

I was about to tell my friend the great lie when the security guard came back to our table. I put my worried face again. "Is he gone?" I asked the centaur with false apprehension.

"Yeah," he replied as if he were so proud of himself for meeting his good deeds quota that night, "I saw to it that he left the building."

"Thank you so much!" I gushed with the utmost sense of false sincerity. Thank you, Dad, for instilling in me the value of community theater. "Yeah, he's such a jerk!"

"You'll be okay when you go home?"

"Oh, we'll be fine." I turned to Eddie and batted my eyes at him, which caught him off guard for a moment. "Won't we, babycakes?" I had been wanting to say that to my friend.

"All right!" The centaur walked away from the table.

There was a short silence until Eddie blurted out, "Babycakes?"

I laughed nervously. I had forgotten to warn him. "Oh, yeah, I told the guard that the elf was my ex and that he was violating the restraining order I had on him. So, I asked him to get rid of him."

Eddie nodded. He was impressed with my ingenuity.

"Nice, but that still doesn't answer why you called me

babycakes?"

"Oh," I said off-handedly, "I told the guard that you're my

boyfriend."

"Gee, I'm flattered that I'm your babycakes," Eddie said as

he gathered up his empty salad plate and half-empty bottle. He

grabbed my tray and dumped the remains in a nearby trash can.

I was sipping my root beer when he sat back down.   He was

staring at my drink, wishing he hadn't accidentally tossed his.

"Thirsty?" I asked him offering my soda.

"I don't drink. . . root beer," he said mysteriously as a

fanged smile flashed across his face.

I resisted the strong temptation to give him a swift kick in

the shin. Eddie knows I hate his lame vampire jokes, but it's

hard to stay mad at him, especially whenever he smiles at me.

Instead, I just rolled my eyes at him. "Knock it off with the

cheesy Dracula voice!"

He only flashed his smile again at me, which made me

swoon inwardly. "So, are we done shopping?" he asked me in

an almost pleading voice.

"One more store, and then we can go," I promised him.

Eddie's forehead hit the tabletop with a loud THUMP! When he looked up at me, it looked like someone had drawn several rows of little X's on his forehead.

"That must have hurt," I said. Eddie hated shopping, unusually this late at night. I would keep my promise. "Let's go to that new department store that opened last weekend," I suggested.

Eddie was rubbing his forehead and wishing he hadn't made that last dumb move. "Tally's?" he asked. "Isn't that really expensive?" he said as he slung our shopping bag over one of his shoulders.

We got up from the table as I shook my head at the shopping-impaired vampire. "Tally's Outlet," I corrected him as we walked by a trashcan where I tossed my empty drink. Slam dunk! "It's an outlet store with expensive clothes at discount prices!"

After a short two-minute walk to the other side of the mall, we entered the huge department store. I made a beeline for the women's section. I was looking for something to go with my cocktail dress, and I found it! I wrapped the white feather boa around my neck. "Eddie, darling, could you please get me another martini?" I said as I pretended to take a smoke on one of those long, thin cigars.

Eddie couldn't hide his smile from me as much as he tried. "You look great. You'd really fit in at any high society party," he said without a hint of sarcasm in his voice. But unless you could read his mind, you could never know if Eddie is serious or not. So that's what I did. I hopped inside his mind and was mildly surprised to learn that he really thought I looked hot tonight, minus the boa, of course. That moment was fleeting, for he sensed me reading his mind and immediately switched to thinking about repairing cars. Curse the ability of vampires to block mind reading attempts! Better luck next time.

"You really think so?" I asked innocently. As if I didn't know what he was thinking earlier. "I'm going to buy it!" I decided. I checked the price tag. Fifteen dollars, definitely within my price range. I looked at Eddie. Now, we needed something that said trillion-dollar playboy, not soda jerk.

Actually, I would like him with any job. Did I just think that? I

grabbed the vampire's hand and practically dragged him over to

the men's department. "Now," I said as I pawed through a rack

of colorful silk shirts, "you are going to need one of these for the

party."

Eddie joined me, and within seconds he held up a scarlet

shirt. "What about this one?" he asked me.

"I like it. Try it on!" I urged.

While Eddie went into the nearby men's dressing room, I

spotted some fancy men's accessories. There were tall silk hats

in almost every color of the rainbow, white gloves that I couldn't

even slip my hand into for fear of smudging, cashmere scarves

that were over ten feet in length, and capes. I pushed aside a

couple of red silk cloaks and pulled out a black one with a high

collar. If capes don't stereotype vampires, I don't know what

does.

I hurried back to the fitting room when Eddie came around

the corner. My jaw dropped stupidly, and I forced it back up

before the vampire would notice me. "You're done?" I asked, surprised.

He looked at me. "Hey, give me my gold chain!" he asked. He put on his necklace and turned to face me. "How do I look?" he asked me honestly.

At this point in the night, any outfit that Eddie wore made him look very handsome. I've always liked him in red. Something about that color singing the praises of his irresistible green eyes puts me somewhere beyond cloud nine. God, I was becoming infatuated with him, and I couldn't stop myself. Not that it was a bad thing. "You look h-nice," I stammered.

"H-nice?" he asked me. I was fortunate that Eddie couldn't read my mind. My secret crush on the sexy vampire was something that he didn't need to know.

"Nothing," I lied. Man, lies were leaking out of me like a Wiffle ball filled with water. Then I handed him the lovely cape. "This is definitely you, Eddie."

"A cape?" Eddie asked, holding it away from him as if it would come alive and bite him. He would never wear one even if someone were holding a gun to his head.

"Come on, you vampires wear capes all the time in the

movies."

"Hmm, yeah, because movies always parallel real life. Shelly, when was the last time you saw me wear a cape?"

I had to think about that one for a moment. "Never?" I ventured.

"Exactly! Capes went out of style with big hair and parachute pants." Eddie folded his arms over his chest, definitely like a spoiled two-year-old. "I won't wear that thing. You can't make me!"

I took the cape back from him. "Drop dead!" I informed the vampire

He went back into the dressing room. and emerged a few minutes later. "Are we done here?" he asked.

"Yep," I said, handing his shopping bag back to him. I looked at all our purchases, including the shirt and boa. "I'd say that we've accomplished a lot tonight."

"Yeah," Eddie replied, "this is exactly how I wanted to spend my evening. Clothes shopping!"

I playfully cuffed the vampire upside the head and quickly strode in front of him so he wouldn't see me smirking. I waited near the exit doors while Eddie paid for our merchandise. He

occasionally rubbed the back of his head while writing out a

check.

92

Chapter 7:

We Nearly Die in a Taxi

"Are you sure this is where we parked?" I asked Eddie for the fifth time in twenty minutes as we scanned the parking lot in the darkness.

The vampire made an affirmative grunt. A worried look spread across his brow. "I remember that we parked near the costume shop entrance," he murmured half to me and half to himself. "Then, where the heck is my motorcycle?"

"Maybe, someone stole it," I suggested and immediately regretted it. Not the smartest thing to say at the moment. "Or got towed?" I said, trying to cover my butt. I looked at Eddie to see his reaction.

He didn't say anything at first. Instead, he left my side and began to scan inch by inch each and every parking space as if he would find some clue to the whereabouts of his precious motorcycle. Suddenly, he picked up a white envelope that shone brightly in the light of the street lamp. It was addressed to the vampire.

I walked over to him while he opened up the envelope. "What does it say?" I asked.

Eddie began to read the letter aloud for my benefit. "'Thank you for your payments, Van Helsing. I expect the rest of the money to be delivered in cash at my home in Rockfort Hills by Sunday evening. Instructions will follow.'" It was written in flourishing, sophisticated handwriting on pale blue stationery. Even though it had no signature at the bottom, Eddie knew precisely who it was from. He swore under his breath, and I couldn't blame him. "I spent three hundred druci on that motorcycle! I can't believe he stole it!"

I could've told Eddie that I wasn't a bit surprised that the Chairman stole his motorcycle and that I wasn't paranoid on our way over here, but I wisely kept my mouth shut. Instead, I was more worried about how we would get home. I hopped inside the vampire's mind to see what he was planning. Now that Stregone had his favorite motorcycle, he was determined to get it back, even if that meant crashing the sorcerer's party on Thursday night. I shook my head in bewilderment. Eddie was more concerned about the well-being of his motorcycle than my paintings that he had inadvertently got stolen.

"So," I asked slowly, "what are we going to do next?"

"I'll call a taxi," he grumbled. Eddie pulled his cell phone off his belt clip and dialed information. "Could you connect with the number of Bob's Pretty Good Taxi, please?" He waited for a few minutes, still fuming silently about his precious motorcycle. "Yeah, we need a taxi here at the Moonlight Mall Main Street entrance. Nothing with wings! Name's Eddie Van Helsing. Fifteen minutes? Thank you!" He put his phone back on the belt clip.

"Bob's Pretty Good Taxi?" I asked him. I had seen this taxi service advertised on television, and Eddie had as well but didn't stick around for the last thirty seconds of the commercial where Bob's passengers were apparently screaming in terror or puking out the windows.

"I like to support up and coming businesses," he replied as we walked over to a nearby bench and sat down.

I set my bags down on the pavement and leaned forward. "So, now you're all geared up to crash the party?" I asked Eddie.

The vampire nodded. "How did you know? Oh, that's

right! You can read my mind!" He sometimes forgets about my magical talent. He leaned forward and cupped his head in his hands in frustration, regretting that he ever got caught up in this mess. "Remind me never to do a favor that involves mob bosses."

"And doesn't involve smelly blue mushroom fuel. Blech!" I made a disgusted face. It reminded me of the toilet bowl cleaner that the dog drank and then expelled on Grandma's ugly braided rug. Just thinking about the fuel inspired a gag reflex. "How can you even use that stuff?"

Eddie looked up at me. A smile ran across his face. "It's supposedly cheap and good for the environment.." Then his tone became serious. ""I'm going to hunt Tony down and kill the little prick."

"Not if I kill him first," I replied. "Does the fuel smell as bad as I think it does?"

Eddie nodded. "It reeks, and it's highly combustible. I used it once, and let's just say that I had no trouble locating the fire extinguisher."

"Good thing you didn't burn down the garage," I said with

a grin.

That brought a smile to Eddie's face as he began chuckling. "Oh, I came very close." His laugh was contagious. Maybe, because it was late at night and I was tired, we both started laughing so hard that we barely felt the hefty thump of our taxi.

Yes, you heard me correctly. I did say thump. Most Zephyr cabs employ in their services a wide variety of transportation choices. If you want to fly, you can ride a dragon, winged horse, or even a giant hornet or dragonfly. For those who prefer to stay close to the ground, a unicorn-pulled carriage is perfect, but the ride we got was not what I wanted to ride after a big meal.

A dwarf in his sixties pulled the reins back on a green and yellow grasshopper that was about the size of a school bus. The insect came to a screeching halt only a foot and a half away from our bench. Strapped to the bug were three captains' chairs with no visible seatbelts. "Yo, man," the dwarf called to Eddie, "you called for a taxi?"

Great! I get to ride a giant grasshopper. The last time I

rode one, I spent the next day wondering if chiropractors have a lot of patients who ride the insects, while I waited for the aspirin for my neck and back pain to kick in. If I wanted to be in a moving bounce house, I would have joined a carnival. I glanced at Eddie. *You don't like to fly, and this is what we get instead?* I asked him mentally.

Eddie shrugged helplessly. *As if I planned this*, he retorted. The vampire finally spoke to the driver, "I called for a taxi!"

You are so paying!

We scaled the fraying rope ladder he threw down to us. I climbed, thanking God that each rung I stepped on hadn't caused me to fall and break my neck. I looked up at Eddie, who practically shot out his arms and yanked me to "safety." I found the seat belt, along with other unrecognizable things, stuffed deep in the cracks of my seat. I tried to close the used airplane clasps together. *Does your seat belt work?* I asked Eddie, who had apparently sat in something blue and sticky.

I haven't found mine yet was his disturbing response. He had tied all our bags together and had put them in between his feet.

"Oh," the driver called to Eddie from the front seat, "the seat belt was giving some people trouble, so I just cut it off."

That's good to know! "Are you going to get it replaced?" I asked, looking around for something to grip for support.

"Nah, too expensive!"

"So, why are you wearing a seat belt?" Eddie asked the question for me.

"Taxi regulations," our penny-pinching driver replied.

Eddie and I exchanged nervous looks. At least our driver will survive. This was not how my vampire friend wanted to spend his second death. Eddie gave the driver our addresses and insisted that I be dropped off first.

I appreciated the vampire's concern for a safe trip home for me, providing the fact, I actually make it home. I heard the dwarf give the reins a hard snap, and the grasshopper lurched forward, nearly giving us whiplash. As we hopped perilously along, I wasn't enjoying the scenery. In fact, my whole life flashed before my eyes, almost making me sick. *I'm going to die, I'm going to die, I'm going to die* was my death mantra as I held the two clasps of the seat belt, praying that if I fell off the beast, the straps would hold. I squeezed my eyes shut.

I stood on my doorstep with my legs still shaking violently. The taxi and Eddie had already left. At my request, Eddie did a quick search of my house in his mist form. I certainly didn't want any unwelcome visitors. My knuckles were turning back to their normal color as I unlocked my door. Even though it was a scary trip home, I was utterly exhausted but proud of myself that I didn't throw up at all.

It was almost three o'clock in the morning, but it was the weekend, so I could sleep in. I stepped inside and tossed my bags on the kitchen table that was cluttered already with the mess that I discovered last night. A shudder ran through my body. I made sure four times that all the windows and doors were locked. "I'll clean up the mess tomorrow!" I told myself as I headed off to bed. My heart beating loudly, I lay in bed, listening for any unusual noises for about an hour before I drifted off to sleep.

Chapter 8:
I Learn about the Process of Cheese
and Stregone's History

I spent the next morning cleaning up my house. Once I was done, I sat down at my computer. I decided to do some online research about Mr. Stregone. As it turned out, Stregone grew up in a small town called San Basilo up in the gorgeous Sancia Mountain range overlooking the Sapphire Sea. I remembered flying Jordan there when I first got her. The rainbow rocks almost danced in the lavender sunset.

According to their website, San Basilo is a farming community, known for their fine wines, such as Snapdragon, Pink Lady, Casablanca Rose, and many others, that they ship all over the world. Their famous scented cheeses, which according to the webpage, "are fit for a king, but reasonable enough for a peasant." Now, I'm not talking about your normal Limburger and cheddar cheese. The cheeses are scented like flowers. Sweet pea, roses, daisies, tulips. You name it, they make it.

As much as I like to read about the cheese-making process, I clicked on a link about the town's history. Six thousand years ago, the wizard Gucci Basilo and his exploration team accidentally discovered the city. According to the legend, Basilo was a geologist on the hunt for rare purple emeralds, but once he found them, he refused to share his wealth with his coworkers. The team left him without food or water. Basilo wandered for eight months, lost in the mountains. Finally, he stumbled into the village where the native elves hailed him as a god. By this point, I found myself nodding off. I slapped myself in the face to keep awake.

Even though I'm a sucker for history, I found it really dull. To fool Stregone, did I really need to know about Basilo's godlike state? I went back to MetaMagic, my favorite search engine, and did a keyword search on "Stregone, Mario." I finally found a website dedicated to the sorcerer's family lavender cheese farm. Don Stregone and his wife and author of the site, Bella, have two sons, Don Jr., and Mario. I clicked on the link under Mario's name. Mommy dearest must have been very proud of her son's accomplishments. Mario graduated summa cum laude both at San Basilo Academy and at Wixom College of Magic. I clicked on the link to Wixom College of Magic and was immediately sent to its website.

Then I had another brilliant idea. I found the link to their alumni and saw a picture of Greta Morgana, a palm reading major who graduated from the same class as Stregone. Apparently, they shared some of the same courses. Without the red hair, she could have been a long lost relative of mine. I could definitely be her, and nobody would be the wiser. After turning on the printer (the last time, I waited thirty minutes for something to print out, and then Robin pointed out to me that I had forgotten to turn on the printer), I printed off the webpage.

I went back to the site about the Chairman and read some more. Stregone went on to WCM's graduate school, and shockingly enough, graduated at the top of his business management class. His first job out of grad school was the assistant manager of Zephyr Realty. Within three years, he became the CEO of the company. I frowned. That was some really fast-moving up the company ladder. I would have to look into that more closely. Stregone had his hands in several charities, such as scholarship funds for underprivileged kids, feeding the poor, and various children's' hospitals.

Then I remembered Robin telling me about the missing police files on the sorcerer. I did a keyword search in the *Zephyr Herald*'s online archive, and ten minutes later, I came upon an article requesting the public to notify the police about any missing files that had been lost on the way to a court hearing to try Stregone for the murder of a local businessman. Detective Angus was transporting the data in a carriage when the unicorns pulling got spooked by a snake that had slithered across the road next to a steep ravine. The carriage had overturned, and Detective Angus blacked out from a major concussion. By the time authorities had gotten there, the files were gone, the minotaur had no recollection of what happened after the crash, and the case was dismissed for lack of evidence. Can't imagine who stole the files.

I rubbed my eyes and checked my watch. It was almost noon. Then I realized that I was meeting Creighton at my dad's for lunch. I quickly ran a comb through my hair, grabbed my purse, and headed out the door. I saddled up Jordan and flew over to the diner.

Creighton was waiting for me inside at a booth. She had her ebony black hair back in a French braid and was wearing a pink flowered shirt that went well with her black horse-like body. "Guess what!" she said the minute I sat down.

"What?" I asked.

Her green eyes sparkled with uncontainable joy. "I've got a date tonight!" she said with a huge smile.

And I'll be sitting at home cutting coupons tonight! Go me! "With who?" I asked.

Creighton pointed to the long, blond hair, blue-eyed centaur taking orders at a nearby table. "Isn't Tanner cute?"

The royal blue uniform did go well with his white flank. He was good-looking for a centaur. "But not as cute as Eddie," I said under my breath. Whoa, did I just say that? *What's wrong with me?* I asked myself. *He's just my best friend.* "He's good-looking," I finally said to her. "When did he ask you out?"

"Well, I saw him the other night, and he was flirting with me a bit. Then I saw him talking to Eddie, and just a few minutes ago, Tanner asked me out tonight! Eddie's such a nice guy, isn't he?"

"Yeah, he's great!" I said with an involuntary smile.

"You like him, don't you!" Creighton asked as if she could read my mind.

"Tanner?"

"You know perfectly well who I'm talking about!"

Tanner came by our table. Saved by the waiter! He grinned at Creighton. "So, can I get you ladies something to drink?" he asked in a charming voice as he pulled out a pad of paper and a pen from his white apron pocket.

"I'll have an iced tea," Creighton said. Her cheeks blushed.

I wanted Eddie's specialty: cream soda with a dash of strawberry, but of course, the vampire wasn't here to serve it to me at the moment. I settled for something else. "I'll take a root beer," I said with a sigh.

"Okay, I'll be back with your drinks," Tanner said. Then he

turned away and trotted off to the kitchen.

"So, what are you going to get for lunch?" I asked my friend as I gazed at my menu. "I think I'm going with the chicken ranch sandwich. What about you?"

Creighton shook her head. "You're avoiding my question, Shelly, but I'll humor you. I'm going to have the alfredo shrimp pasta dish. Now, are you going to answer me?"

I sighed. "Okay, I wish I knew how I felt. Lately, I've been unsure about my feelings towards Eddie." It felt really great to get those feelings out in the open, especially with my best girlfriend.

Creighton looked at me, quizzically. "So, what exactly are your feelings towards him?" She folded her hands together and rested her chin on top of them. Apparently, she had been putting those freshman-level psychology courses to use.

"Okay!" I took in a deep breath of air. "I have a crush on him."

"Really?"

"I know it sounds crazy. He's one of my best friends and all." I told her a little bit about shopping last night with Eddie, but I didn't tell her that we were planning to crash a mafia boss' party on Thursday night. "I was staring at him like a deer in headlights! What is wrong with me, Creighton?"

"You're in love with him."

I easily avoided the topic at hand because Tanner came back with our drinks and took our orders. Once he was out of earshot, I continued our conversation. "Okay, I'm falling in love with him, but I'm not sure if he feels the same way."

"Have you tried reading his mind?" Creighton asked as she bit into her pasta.

"Oh, please, you know that vampires can block mind-reading," I said. Then I smiled. "But I did catch a little bit. He thought that I looked really nice in this red wig."

"A wig?"

"Yeah, we were just acting silly." I didn't like lying to the centaur, but then again, she didn't need to get involved with the Board of Directors. "What should I do?" I finally asked. I was trying to keep my trembling body under control. Whenever I talk to someone about my deepest feelings, I start to shake and get really nervous for some unknown reason. I think it might be because I rarely tell, even my closest friends, my deepest thoughts and secrets. Believe me, my feelings towards Eddie had been a closely guarded secret until now.

Tanner arrived with our food, and we quickly stopped talking. Once he had left, Creighton spoke up. "I think you should tell Eddie your feelings."

"Are you serious?" I was taken aback by her suggestion. "I mean, I don't want to lose the friendship that I have with him if he doesn't feel the same way." My lips were dry, so I sipped my root beer. My food was getting cold, and there's nothing that I hate more than a chicken sandwich going through a second Ice Age. I took a bite, and a massive glob of honey mustard fell on the edge of the table, missing the fourteen-dollar shirt that I picked up at the Dollar Days at the Moonlight Mall last year with Gemini. Using my napkin to wipe up the mess, I changed the subject. "So, what are you and Tanner planning on doing tonight?"

"I think probably dinner and an outdoor movie. I think he's going to take me to that fancy new restaurant on Sycamore Avenue. What's it called?" She snapped her fingers as she tried to recall the name.

"Orchidée?" I took another bite from my sandwich.

The centaur nodded excitedly. As we ate, we talked about my art exhibits (I didn't mention the fact that a mafia henchman stole them from me to pay off Eddie's debts), her hospital rounds, and of course, Tanner. I made sure that the conversation never turned to my crush on Eddie.

Chapter 9:

I Do Some Kung Fu Fighting

The sun had sunk low in the sky as I walked home from the nearby grocery store. I had run out of milk and cereal that morning and had just remembered to buy them not too long ago. The pale purple moon had almost grown to its fullest. Suddenly, I got a weird feeling that I was being followed again. I could pick up some brain waves. A werewolf was just a few feet behind me. Tonight was a full moon, and that meant pack night for all Weres. Pack meetings, from what Gemini and Tucker have told me, usually are pretty much like town meetings. The topics range from Saturday's bake sale to next Friday nights' softball games to city politics. Sometimes, a Were from out of town will come to be a guest speaker. Raquel's brother-in-law, the mute poet, Milton, had a book signing one time. All Weres eighteen and over are required to attend these meetings. So, why wasn't this guy at his pack meeting?

A sudden grip of fear ran over me as I read the man's mind. The creep was going to kidnap me and have Eddie pay the Chairman ransom money for my "safe" return. Yeah, and monkeys can write Shakespeare! I prepared myself for a possible attack as I started to pick up my pace.

The werewolf suddenly grabbed my left elbow with a hairy hand. The sleeve of my favorite shirt tore with a loud RIP! He pulled me close to him. "What a pretty prize you'll be!" he snarled with his wretched doggy breath in my face.

The milk fell out of my hands and splattered all over the sidewalk, which made me furious. That was the last bottle of milk at the store, and there was no way that I was going to another store. Now, my dad's a second-degree black belt in karate, and he taught both Robin and me some self-defense moves in case we were ever attacked. Without giving the guy any warning, I sucker-punched him under the chin with my free hand and tried to run away from him, but I tripped, falling to the ground. The contents of my purse scattered across the sidewalk.

He staggered back, stunned that this "helpless" human girl had such a tremendous punch. But the bugger was resilient. He charged at me. A bad mistake on his part.

It doesn't matter what you are, a satyr, elf, vampire, or even a werewolf. If you're a member of the male species, a good, swift kick below the belt is going to hurt. And that's what I did. "Get away from me!" I ordered him.

The werewolf gave a loud, but wimpy howl as he doubled over in pain. He called me an unkind name. I scooped up my belongings and made a run for it down the street. "Come on, Shelly!" I told myself as my lungs started to ache. I could hear my heart thumping in my chest. Find a weapon, Shelly. My keys! That will work! I quickly inserted a key between each finger on my right hand. I glanced over my shoulder as a big black shadow leaped at me. He just wouldn't give up! I whirled around and thrust my keyed fist into the side of his face. He howled in pain as blood gushed out from his nose and cheek. "I said, get away from me, you creep!" I screamed. I kicked high and hard this time. A couple of ribs cracked, and he screamed in intense pain.

"You heard her! Back off!" I looked up to see Eddie standing right beside me. He was holding a sharp, silver throwing knife at his side. He was actually enjoying seeing me beating the snot out of the Were. "I wouldn't come near her again if I were you."

The werewolf nodded, still holding his bloody face. He turned away from us, and we watched him limp through a brick wall. I turned to the vampire once I was able to catch my breath. "You missed all the action."

Eddie smiled. "I don't want to get on your bad list. You pack quite a punch!" He bent down and picked up my cell phone. It must have fallen out of my purse during the fight. "You okay?" he asked as he put an arm around my shaking body.

I looked down at the blood dripping off my keys and onto my knuckles. My arm was going to hurt like heck later on tonight. "Yeah, I'm fine. Great timing, though!"

"I was taking a walk before I headed into work, and I saw

you kick the crap out of that guy. I assume he wasn't looking for your autograph." Eddie led me over to a nearby bench.

"No, the Chairman had paid him to kidnap me and force you to pay the ransom money," I told him what happened, blushing a little bit as I realized how concerned Eddie was for my safety. Maybe Creighton was right, I should let Eddie know how I feel about him. I was about to explain my infatuation to him when he asked me where I learned those kick-butt moves. "My dad taught me karate growing up. I improvised with the keys."

"You've got to teach me those moves someday!" Eddie got up from his seat, and we walked to a convenience store down the block. He listened intently as I told him what I had discovered on the Internet, and the best thing was that he never interrupted me. After I was done chatting, he finally spoke. "Think it'll work?"

I shrugged. "It's worth a try, but at the party, let me do most, if not all the talking. I don't want the Chairman to recognize you." The last thing I wanted was to be pulling a wooden stake out of the vampire's chest. We stood in line to pay for another jug of milk for me. Eddie took some cash out of his wallet and paid the cashier.

Just another slow night at Anderson's Place. I could tell because Dad was out front wiping off the counter when Eddie and I came into the diner. He looked up at us. "Eddie, you're here early—," Dad started to say when he saw the blood on my hand. "Shelly, what happened?" he asked as he practically leaped over the island. "Why is there blood all over your hand?"

"Some punk werewolf tried to mug me, Dad!" I explained as he wiped the remaining blood off my wrist. The quicker, thicker picker-upper, Bounty! I was tempted to hum the jingle. "Don't worry, I fought him off," I said, winking at Eddie.

"Yeah, Mr. Anderson," Eddie exclaimed, "you should've seen Shelly kick that werewolf's butt!"

Dad looked at me, curiously. "I did what you taught me," I replied. "And just to clear away your worries, he didn't bite me."

Just then, my dad's forty-three-year-old girlfriend came out of the kitchen. "Timothy, honey," Amelia started to say, but the second she saw me, she gave a small gasp. "Shelly, what happened to your shirt?" she asked.

"I was nearly mugged by this werewolf, Amelia," I explained. I felt terrible about the shirt. Amelia had given it to me for my birthday last year. "I think he was on drugs or something."

"Not to worry, Miss Cross." Eddie put his hand on my shoulder. "The Karate Kid here almost killed him." He pretended to go into a move out of *Crouching Tiger, Hidden Dragon.*

Amelia shook her hand at the vampire. "Still, let me make sure he didn't hurt you, Shelly," she said, giving me the once over. She used to be an RN, and so she can spot an injury a mile away.

"I'm fine!" I protested. "In fact, I think I broke a couple of his ribs."

"Well," Dad said as he leaned over the counter to toss the bloody paper towel in a trash can, "at least, you weren't hurt."

Not yet, I thought to myself.

Dad rubbed his chin thoughtfully. "It's a full moon, so I wonder why he wasn't at his pack meeting?"

I shrugged. "Delinquent?" I offered the lie out like candy, hoping someone would bite. "Don't worry about calling the police. I don't think the guy's going to be mugging anyone anytime soon."

Yeah, he'll just rip our spleens out Thursday night. The vampire's encouraging thoughts floated into my mind. Eddie always sees the glass half full.

Ixnay! I told him. "I guess I should be going home," I told everyone as I started to go near the door.

"Wait!" Eddie looked at Dad. "I'll walk Shelly home if you don't mind, Mr. Anderson," he offered.

Dad nodded. "That's a good idea, Eddie. I really don't like the idea of Shelly walking home at night by herself."

The vampire agreed and grabbed my arm that was now black and blue from where the werewolf had caught me. Once we were outside the building, he looked at me. "Nice lie, you told your dad there."

"It wasn't a lie!" I protested.

"Then, what was it? Enlighten me, please."

"Let me give you the rubber band theory," I explained. I pulled on an imaginary elastic band with my thumbs and index fingers. "Truth is like a rubber band. You can stretch it out as far as you like it or until it snaps."

"So, when it snaps, the truth becomes a lie?"

"Exactly!"

Eddie gave me a skeptical look. "B-B-Bull crap!"

I shrugged. "Argue with Robin. He invented the theory. What did you expect me to tell my dad and Amelia? 'Guess what, Dad? I was almost abducted because Eddie's in serious debt with a mob boss. They were going to use my ransom money as a debt reduction plan.' That would've gone over really well with them."

"I'd probably be without a job right about now, or he would've killed me 'cause I put you in danger."

I laughed. "Yeah, Dad's pretty protective of me." *And so are you, Eddie,* I thought to myself. Then a little voice that sounded a lot like Billy Joel started singing in my head, "Tell him about it. Tell him everything you feel. Give him every reason to accept that you're for real. Tell him about it. Tell him all your crazy dreams." Now's not the time, Piano Man. I'll tell him about it later. "So, we need to devise a plan for Thursday night."

Eddie nodded. "I thought that I could meet you at your place around six, and then have a taxi take us to Rockfort Hills."

"Great idea! I will wow the Chairman with my strong resemblance to one of his classmates from college. I will read palms."

"You do realize that you will be impersonating a Welkie," Eddie reminded me as we walked down my street. "And last time I checked, you don't know any magic."

"I can read minds."

"Undead minds," my friend corrected.

I could almost hear my plans to rescue the paintings and the motorcycle being flushed down the proverbial toilet. "Crap! That's not going to work! Unless there's a couple of vampires or werewolves at this party. Other than you, Eddie, of course."

"I know a little magic. I could help you out if you want."

We had arrived at my front door. The security light flickered on, which helped me out as I inserted my house key in the doorknob. I smiled at Eddie as I opened the door. "Thanks, you're the best!"

"No problem."

He started to go when I said, "Uh, Eddie—."

The vampire turned to look at me. "What is it?"

What I wanted to say was, "I have feelings for you, and I'm falling in love with you. I think the feelings are mutual, but you guard your thoughts so well that I'm not sure what you think about me." But actually, it came out like, "Well, have a good night at work. See you Thursday night." I waved good-bye to Eddie and watched him walked away in the light of the full moon. I locked my door and hit my head against one of the window panes. *Stupid, Shelly!* I scolded myself. *You had the chance to tell him how you feel, and you screwed it up!* What was wrong with me? Then I thought about what I had wanted to say to him. I probably was being a little direct with my feelings. Most likely, I would've scared Eddie to a second death if I actually told him my short speech. If the opportunity arises again, I promised myself, I would be more tactful.

Chapter 10:
We Crash the Party, Kind of

The next few days went by without much action. No werewolves trying to grab me and no unnecessary lying to cover my butt. Overall, it was reasonably quiet until Thursday night. I decided not to wear my cocktail dress because I did not want to ruin it in case we did any running for our lives. Instead, I ironed a pair of black pants that I found stuffed at the bottom of one of my dresser drawers and threw them on. Then I pulled on a purple silk dress shirt. I put on the red wig that Eddie thought I looked really cute in, tucking in brown strands of hair. To add the finishing touch, I put on the fake pearl necklace and chic boa and admired myself in the mirror. Boy, what would Eddie think when he saw me? I looked good if I did say so myself.

I didn't have to wait long for the vampire to come by precisely at six o'clock. He came inside and gave a low whistle when he took one look at me and my silly outfit. "You look really cute tonight," he said honestly. He helped himself to a glass of fruit juice in the fridge.

I smiled at him for three reasons. One, I knew he was telling the truth. Number two, he looked absolutely hot in his red silk shirt with the first three buttons undone and his gold chain necklace resting on his bare chest. Reason number three, I was trying not to laugh out loud at the poofy wig he was wearing. "So, do you. Without the wig, of course." I followed Eddie to the kitchen table, where he unfolded a piece of paper that he pulled out his pants pocket.

"I managed to get a copy of the blueprints of Rockfort Hills Estate," he told me as I studied the plans. He pointed to a large area marked garage. "I think that Stregone might have the paintings and motorcycle here. Stregone and I have conducted business in there."

"You mean 'Stregone has collected the money you owe him.'" I corrected him.

Eddie merely nodded and continued. "As I was saying, it's fairly easy to hide something as big as a motorcycle."

"Are you sure? I mean, I've ridden by Rockfort Hills, and

the place is big enough to hide at least a hundred Mac trucks."

Eddie studied the map for another minute or so. "I guess we'll have to look in every room ourselves." Then he looked at me curiously. "Let's clear one thing up. Is what we are doing legal?"

"If he invites us into his home, then yes, it's legal. One may consider snooping around unethical, but certainly not against the law."

"I was afraid you would say that." The vampire looked around for my phonebook, and once I grabbed it from the top of the refrigerator (don't ask!), he flipped through the green-colored pages for the number to Zephyr Carriage Taxi. Apparently, Bob's Pretty Good Taxi wasn't good enough for him. He dialed the number and asked for a unicorn-drawn carriage here to be in a few minutes.

The ride to Rockfort Hills was uneventful, which was a good thing, considering the last taxi ride we had. The elf driving the platinum carriage came to a stop under an eight skylight overhang. Eddie was fortunate enough to be able to discreetly pay the driver, and said to him, "Thank you, James!" as we got out.

I breathed in deeply. Steady, girl. There's nothing to be afraid of. You're just going to crash a mob boss' party. I glanced over at my escort, who was secretly hoping that we would survive the night. We approached the burly satyr dressed in all black who was checking IDs at the door. "Excuse me, let us through, please!" I asked in my best high society accent. It was that or my Peter Loree impression, which would have been *so* inappropriate at the time.

"Do you have an invitation?" the bouncer snarled at us. Apparently, we weren't on his favorite people list, which I would suspect not too many people were.

"Actually, Mario never sends me an invitation!" I said, turning up my nose at the satyr. My eyes swept the crowd until I spotted the Welkie drinking a martini with a couple of his business associates. I began to wave furiously. "Mario, baby! Remember me?" I called over the hum of the crowd.

Stregone turned to study me with his muddy brown eyes. His gray hair was perfectly combed off to the left side of his head without a strand out of place. He finally came over to the front door. "Do I know you?" he asked me.

"Of course, you would forget! It's been so long! I'm Greta Morgana!" I said loud enough for everyone to hear. If I put up a fuss that everyone could listen to, he would have to let Eddie and me in.

"Greta Morgana?"

"I sat three rows behind you in freshman History of Magic class at Wixom College of Magic with Dr. Merlin!"

A light of recognition seemed to go on over the sorcerer's head. "Ah, yes! Now, I remember! What brings you here?"

"Well, I was traveling through Zephyr with my bodyguard, Rusty here," I jerked my thumb towards Eddie, who quickly put on a poker face. "And I heard that you live here. So, I said to myself, 'Self, let's go visit Mario so that we could catch up on old times.'"

Stregone looked flustered for a moment. "Well, as you can see, Miss Morgana, I'm having a social gathering at the moment. Perhaps, we can chat some other time."

I put my hands on my hips. "That's just not good, Mario! I

leave early tomorrow morning for my next palm reading, and I'm booked for the next year and a half!"

Stregone shrugged helplessly. "You may come in. My house is your house," he told us warmly as he had me sit down at a nearby table. Eddie stood behind me and acted his role as a bodyguard perfectly. I tried not to look at him for help. I had to execute my next move smoothly. "Why don't I try reading your palm, Mario?" I suggested.

The sorcerer sat down across from me and held out his palm. "So, you've really got this palm reading down to a fine art, have you, Greta?" he asked me.

"Been working on it for over ten years," I replied with a forced smile. I ran my fingers along the lines of his palm. I began to murmur some mumbo jumbo when, to my surprise, a little pale blue ball of energy slowly floated over the table. "I sense that you are having money trouble."

Stregone leaned forward with interest. "Really? Can you tell me what kind of trouble?" he asked.

I paused for a moment, trying to rack my brain. The last thing I needed was to accidentally blow our cover. "Somebody owes you money."

"When will he give it to me?"

"I don't know." Slowly, the floating ball began to fade. "I can't see your future right now because the channel's getting all fuzzy."

Stregone wrenched his hand away. "How is that possible?" he thundered. Then he realized that everyone was staring at him. "I mean, why does the channel fade in and out?"

I frantically racked my brain for an answer. Then Eddie came up with one. *Tell him that the channel to the future is like a washing machine. It spins and churns, sometimes fading the colors of life.* Nice philosophical piece of crap, Eddie, but that was all I had to work with at the moment. I relayed the message to the mob boss.

"Hmmm," Stregone said. He beckoned to a scantily dressed female vampire. "Trixie, come over here!" Then he looked at me. "Can you tell my friend's future?"

I smiled with all the confidence in the world. "Of course, I can." Stregone gave his seat to the blond hair vampire. She looked at me as I slowly drifted into her mind. Stregone was one of her highest paying clients. No, she wasn't a doctor. Her pimp beat her up, and now she was going to ask Stregone to take care of him. I looked up to see another blue ball of energy hover above the table. Eddie's magic was making my career as a medium work perfectly. "Trixie, you've been in a series of relationships, but your last relationship didn't go well, did it?"

Trixie clapped her hands together. "Oh, you are the best fortune teller I have ever met." She leaned across the table. "That vampire you have with you is pretty hot! Can I do him?"

I was shocked for a moment, but I recovered quickly. "Can't. He's a eunuch!" I heard a small involuntary choke coming from Eddie.

For the next half hour, I "read" minds. The elf, Drake Elfstone, had just taken off his wedding ring and was looking for another woman in his life. I overheard a fairy telling someone that she had just come into some money, and I made a wild guess that an enchantress's house caught on fire last week (when I just smelled the smoke off her clothes). I knew that I couldn't keep up all this lucky guessing any longer. I stood up. "Mario!" I asked the sorcerer, "where is your restroom?"

Mario smiled at me. "Down the middle hall, fourth door on your left."

I nodded my thanks as Eddie and I made our way down the central hall lined with blue and white stripes. Then we made a sharp turn into an open doorway leading to another hall. I jiggled the lock on the first door, but it was tight as a drum.

"Let me try," Eddie said in a voice barely above a whisper. He turned himself into a green mist and darted under the door as if he was being pushed by a sudden wind. A few tense moments flew by until he opened the door for me.

The large library was filled wall to wall with shelves of books. A brown high back leather armchair sat in the middle of the room with a matching footstool in front of it. With the tips of my fingers, I turned on the lamp that was on the small triangular-shaped table located on the right side of the chair. An eerie white glow created dancing shadows across the room for only a moment. There was no other furniture in the room. I began rapping on the spines of several books. Then I skipped a bookcase and rapped on a couple of books again.

"What are you doing?" Eddie asked me.

"Seeing if there's a secret passageway. You know, like in the movies."

"I highly doubt it." He glanced around the room for a minute or two and then took the blueprints out of his pocket. "Let's just see if there are any passageways in the library." He held the paper up to the light. "The library, where we are is here, and I don't see any way out of here except through the door we came in."

I did another look around to see if my paintings were hiding somewhere. I lifted up the seat cushion on a whim. Nothing. "Let's look somewhere else."

"Good idea," Eddie replied as he folded up the paper again. He had me go out the door first, and once he locked it from the inside, he materialized and appeared back in the hallway.

This was our process for the next five rooms. Eddie would turn into mist, slide under the door, and unlock it for me. We would look around, find nothing, and leave the same way we came in without altering the appearance of the room itself. No one could ever tell that someone had actually been in there. The only good thing about our search was that I now knew the living room with the plasma screen television was smack dab in the middle of the two libraries, and that Stregone's weight room was right next to the second bathroom on your left. This information was about as useful as reading a 900-page thesis paper on the psychology behind Michael Jackson's various nose jobs. Finally, we came to the sixth room, and I let out a quiet whoop of praise, for it was the last room in the hall.

I waited patiently for Eddie to unlock the door from the inside, and then I walked into a long rectangular room filled up by one large oval-shaped table lined with several swivel chairs on each side. This probably was where the Board of Directors conducted their nasty business. I gasped the second I saw the faint red splotch on the top of the table. That scene from *The Untouchables,* where Robert DeNiro beats a guy's head in with a baseball bat at a meeting of his cronies, flashed before my mind. "Is that blood?"

Eddie pressed his nose against the table and inhaled deeply. He shook his head. "It's just paint," he assured me, gently touching my arm. Vampires know the difference between blood and paint just by the smell, and I trust Eddie's judgment completely. "Come on, let's keep looking." He pulled me away from the spot, and we walked toward the head of the table where he spotted a closet on the opposite wall. He checked to see if the door would open, and to his amazement, it swung open. There was a small safe.

"Can you open it?" I asked, forgetting about the little scare.

The vampire got down on one knee. "I think so," he replied as he took a tiny briefcase that was about the same size as his wallet. He placed it on the floor and whispered so softly that I had to lean in to actually hear him, "Maximize Five."

I watched in awe as the bag slowly grew to the size of a standard briefcase. "Where did you learn that?" I asked, getting on my knees on the hardwood floor.

Eddie grinned at me. "Shop class?" he replied nonchalantly as he opened up the bag so that it laid out flat on the floor.

I peered inside and was amazed at what I saw. A set of three silver throwing knives, four wooden stakes, four retractable throwing stars (two wood and two silver), two high-powered laser pistols, the best in the class, and several rounds of laser bullets were all neatly arranged inside the briefcase. "Are all of these from your James Bond days?" I asked Eddie as he slipped on a pair of black gloves.

"And when I was a bounty hunter," he responded as he unzipped a side pocket and pulled out a collapsible glass. I could tell that Eddie didn't want to talk about his old jobs. He placed the cup on the door of the metal safe and spun the dial a few times. Finally, we heard the click, and the vampire pulled the door opened.

"What is it?" I asked.

Eddie began to leaf through the stack of papers. "They look like bills of some sort," he replied as he handed me half of them. "Oh, here we go. An order form for blue mushrooms."

I glanced over his shoulder. It was a yellow piece of paper with Stregone's signature, allowing six boxes of blue mushrooms sent to his homes. "Should we take it with us?" I asked him.

He shook his head. "I've got a better idea. Get the pen camera out of the third pocket next to the wooden stakes."

I carefully avoided brushing my fingertips across the spikes and pulled out an all too familiar pen cam with the initials R.D.A. in engraved on the side. "Hey, this is Robin's. Dad got it for him two Christmases ago. Why do you have it?" I asked.

Eddie looked up from his browsing and hesitated for a moment. "Oh, that? I borrowed it from Robin a few days ago. I thought that maybe we could gather some evidence, and then I'm turning the photos over to the police." He still hadn't figured out how he was going to explain all of this to them, but at least he had a plan.

"Good thinking. You didn't tell Robin what you were going to do with it, did you?"

The vampire shook his head. He found some other papers, one with Detective Angus's hush money payments, along with the missing police files. He took the camera from me and snapped several pictures. Once they were developed, he was going to drop them off anonymously at the police. He placed the camera back in the briefcase, closed it up, and said the magic word. "Minimize One!" The bag shrank back down to its original size, and he slipped it into his pocket.

"Well, it's good to see you again, Mr. Van Helsing and Miss Anderson!"

We both turned around to see Stregone flanked by his two henchmen, the Treasurer and the Secretary. My friend and I had no idea how long they had been standing there. For some silly reason, I imagined the mob boss wrapped up in a giant Persian rug and saying, "I would've gotten away with it, too, if it hadn't been for you meddling kids."

Instead, the Chairman threw back his arms and shouted, "Slumber!" A cloud of sparkling dust hit Eddie and me head-on. My eyelids felt like baby elephants as I strained to keep them open. Big, fuzzy shapes moved toward us. Where was Eddie? Why was I so tired all of a sudden? I could barely hear Stregone say, "Take them to the garage" before I quickly nodded off to the land of dreams.

Chapter 11:

We Play Tag with Gargoyles

I find myself lying flat on my back, staring up at a white ceiling. My arms feel like cement as I try to shield my face from the bulbs bright enough to guide ships to land in a foggy storm. The room, I guess that's where I am, is round with light blue bunnies and pale green ducks—singing and dancing? Yes, they are actually doing the hokey pokey against a stunningly white background. It is like listening to Alvin and the Chipmunks on acid. Suddenly, I see an old man with a long white beard and dressed like a monk dancing above me. He reachedsinto a paper bag and tosses out handfuls of dry sand while singing at the top of his lungs, "Are you sleeping, Brother John?"

I try to open my mouth to scream for the singing to stop, but nothing comes out. What is the heck is going on?

Suddenly, I hear a loud bang, and a green cloud of smoke fills the room. It dissipates, and Eddie stands beside me. At least, I think it's Eddie. He's wearing a large black cape with the collar sticking up higher than his head. The white and black

tuxedo make him look like a cross between a penguin and

Grandpa from The Munsters. He kneels beside me and says with

a terrible Peter Loree impression, "Get up! For tonight we feast!

Are you awake, my queen? Wake up!" His creepy voice starts to

fade away. "Shelly, get up!"

Something hit the back of my head. "I'm up! I'm up!" I said as if I were on fire. I opened my eyes to complete darkness. I was lying on my side on a cold concrete floor. Someone was lying next to me with his back up next to me. I was picking up some sort of brain waves, but I was finding it difficult to tell who it was because of my grogginess. I tried to move my arms and found that they were handcuffed behind my back. My wig and feathery boa were gone as well.

"You okay, Shelly?" I heard Eddie's voice in the darkness.

"Yeah," I replied, "something hit me on the head." I tried to sit up but to no avail. Something was weighing me down.

"Sorry, that was me. I kind of head-butted you backward."

"And I was having the best dream, too," I replied

sarcastically.

"Really? 'Cause the dream I had was like taking an acid trip!"

"Mine, too," I told him my dream (excluding the part where he came in and called me his queen). "What happened?"

"Stregone hit us with a sleeping spell. These spells cause someone to fall asleep without warning. If they don't wake up in three hours, the spell can't be broken, and the person will die in their sleep. I had to wake you up."

"How come you woke up first?"

"The spell doesn't work very well on vampires. Now, let's see about getting us out of here. Can you sit up?"

"Can't. Something is weighing me down. How about you?"

I felt my body rise a little when Eddie moved. He came down on the floor with a thud. "Same here," he said. Then his fingers brushed against mine, and he cursed under his breath. He told me what I already knew. "We're handcuffed to each other, Shelly."

I broke the long silence. "How are we going to get out of

here?" I asked, more to myself than to Eddie. Then I remembered something. I was handcuffed to a vampire. "Can't you just turn into mist and slip out of these?"

Eddie snorted. "If I could, we wouldn't be having this conversation. These cuffs are magic restricting."

Now, it was my turn to curse. "Crap!" I attempted to look around for something that would actually help us, but then I remembered how bad my night vision is. Probably the best thing to do right now is trying to sit up straight. Later I would try to pick open the lock, and then we would escape safe and sound. "Eddie, let's see if we can sit up straight. Put your elbow on the ground."

Eddie shuffled a bit in his bonds, and finally said, "Got it."

I dug my elbow into the cement. "On the count of three, we pull ourselves up together!"

"One. Two. Three!" We said at the same time. Our bodies went up about four feet and came crashing back down. My shoulder hit the pavement hard. That was going to leave a mark. I couldn't give up. "Again!" I ordered. We did it a second time, but nothing happened, except that my shoulder hurt much worse than before. A third and fourth time. Each time, pain shot up and down my shoulder. I lay on the frosty floor, tears blurring my vision. This was just great. My grand escape idea had failed entirely. Now, I was trapped, God knows where, and there was nothing that I could do. I wasn't Buffy or Anita Blake for that matter. I was just an idiot who wanted to get her paintings back. I stifled a sob.

"Shelly, are you okay?" Eddie asked me.

"No, I'm not okay! My shoulder hurts, and I am handcuffed in a dark room!"

"Let's try getting up again. This time on my count."

"What's the point?"

"Excuse me if I sound selfish, but I don't really like the idea of being Stregone's prisoner. And neither do you." He paused for a moment, and then said softly, "I care a lot about you. For us to get out of here alive, we need to work together. I would rather work with you than with anyone else."

My fears about Eddie's feelings were washed away in that moment. All in one thought, he raised my hopes and told me his feelings. As my dad likes to say, "Suck it up, soldier!" I braced my sore elbow on the ground. "Ready!" I said with gritted teeth and determination.

"One."

"Two."

"Three!" We shouted as we heaved our bodies as one mass up into the air for a third time. No! I told myself as we started to fall back. Then Eddie shifted his weight the opposite way, and with a grunt, we were sitting upright. If I could have kissed the vampire, I probably would have. With all the adrenalin pumping, I hardly noticed the tiny pricking in my butt. "Ow!" I said.

Eddie turned his head towards me. "What's wrong?"

"I'm sitting on something sharp." I lifted my left side a bit and felt around for the item with my fingertips. My friend's back hit mine with a soft thump. "Sorry, Eddie!" I apologized as I managed to grasp the object between my index and middle finger. "It feels like a piece of wire."

"Oh, good! That's just what we need. Some electrical work done."

I ignored Eddie's remarks as I cautiously moved the wire

to my thumb and index finger. With my other fingers, I felt along the base of the cuffs until I found a keyhole. Knowing that I would promptly forget where it was, I awkwardly placed a finger over the hole. "Bingo!"

"What are you doing, Shelly?"

"Trying to pick open the lock."

"You know how to do that?"

I nodded, and then realizing that he probably couldn't see me, I said, "Yep!" I inserted the wire into the keyhole. "When my brother and I were little, my mom used to home-school us. We would get bored easily because there were no other kids our age in our neighborhood." I twisted the wire a couple of times with the two fingers that were holding it. "So, Robin and I would practice escaping from handcuffs."

"Let me guess. Picking open locks was *not* a part of your studies."

I smiled. "We were bored at the time." Suddenly, I heard a satisfying click. Instinctively, I moved both of my arms forward, and so did Eddie. Only the left arm was free.

"One hand's free!" the vampire shouted with triumph. I

could hear the rattle of the handcuffs. "I think we're still handcuffed to each other. You freed my right hand."

This means that Stregone had crisscrossed our handcuffs so that our arms were bound opposite each other, I thought to myself, *Uh, oh! Why don't I feel the wire anymore?* I looked into the blackness in shock. "Eddie, I dropped the wire."

There was a stony silence until he said, "Reach into my back left pocket and pull out my wallet. I think it's still there."

I had to scoot around for a bit until I was facing Eddie's back. I did as I was instructed and pulled out his leather wallet. "Got it. Now what?"

"Open it up. There should be a toothpick in the pocket where I keep my dollar bills."

Have you ever tried to open a wallet when you are handcuffed to another person? It's not as easy as it sounds. I placed the wallet in Eddie's cuffed hand and told him not to move. With my free hand, I opened up the billfold and felt around for the toothpick. I pricked my finger on the tip. "Found it!" I pulled it out. "I hope this hasn't been used."

"It's clean," Eddie assured me. "Now, see if you can pick

open the lock. My butt's getting numb from all this sitting."

"At least you have protection on your butt," I replied as I laid the toothpick in the palm of my cuffed hand. "My knees are starting to ache from kneeling on this cement" I felt around for the keyhole, and once I found it, I retrieved the toothpick and began to work away. In less than two minutes, Eddie was able to slip out of his handcuffs, which meant two things: One, we were free from each other, and two, we still had handcuffs dangling off our wrists like bracelets. It was easier this time, and finally, Eddie chucked the two pairs of handcuffs against the wall with all of his vampire strength that he had regained. "Now, what?"

Eddie got on his knees and pulled out his little black kit. "Maximize 5!" he said in a low voice. There was a slight pause, and I heard him unzip the bag.

Suddenly, I found myself staring into the beam of Eddie's flashlight. I shielded my eyes from the bright light. "Holy cow, Eddie! What kind of bulb is in that thing? The same ones that they use in lighthouses?"

He grinned as he told the bag to minimize again. I was glad that he wasn't wearing that awful wig anymore. Stregone had picked some desperate trophies. Then the vampire got up onto his feet. "Let's find a way out of here," he said as he gently took my wrist.

When Eddie shone the flashlight around, the room we were in was a lot bigger than I had expected. It was about as big as a warehouse. Boxes of all shapes and sizes were piled high. I noticed a couple piles of paintings but decided that it probably wasn't the smartest thing to go rifling through anything in a dark, scary place that you had never been before. Freaky-looking marble creatures with enormous wings were scattered over the room, staring at us with unblinking eyes. It looked like someone getting ready to have a yard sale.

The beam landed on a circuit breaker, and Eddie walked over to it, with me following close behind. He hit a couple of random switches, and parts of the room lit up. "At least, we have a little bit of light. Oh, look! I can see the garage door!" He pointed to a massive door on the other side of the room. Then he nearly broke into a run when he saw his motorcycle next to it. But he stopped short when we both saw a shadow swoop over our heads. He followed it with the beam of the flashlight. The thing was perched on a rafter right above the bike.

As I looked closely at the crouching creature, I saw that it was made of stone, but alive. It looked like a furless monkey with webbed feet, but the similarities stopped there. I could see its huge talon-like hands gripping the rafter. Its gigantic leather wings pulsated silently as the long, spiked tail swished back and forth. Its red eyes glared at us from a distorted bat-like head. A smaller one landed near it, showing its long fangs. Now, you might think, why was I so scared? Here I was digging my fingernails into someone with fangs who happened to be the nicest guy around. But the fangs of these moving statues were dripping with blood. "Eddie, I whispered in a shaky voice, "What are those things?"

"Gargoyles," he whispered. "Don't move! Welkies can make them come alive, providing they aren't exposed to fire."

"What happens when they do?"

"They will explode. Gargoyles are illegal to own because they are very dangerous and extremely strong. They can tear off the head of a dragon with one swipe of their paw."

"How come they haven't attacked us yet?"

"Gargoyles can sense movement. That's how they capture their prey. As long as we stay where we are, they won't attack."

"We can't stay here forever."

"I know. Read my mind."

I drifted into his mind. He had a plan. He was going to blast the two gargoyles with his nebulae spell (whatever that was). Then when they were down, we'd make a run for the motorcycle. I only hoped it would work.

"Nebulae!" Eddie shouted as two huge, flaming balls of scorching white fire shot out from his hands. They whipped towards our guards at warp speed. The gargoyles gave ear piercing, unearthly shrieks as the blast hit them in the stomachs. Then, they exploded with an earth-shattering BOOM! "Run!" the vampire ordered me.

I sprinted to the motorcycle with Eddie on my heels. I could hear massive amounts of wing flapping and loud war cries. Not a good sign! The vampire threw open the garage door with all his strength. A chilly night breeze swept in through the garage. "There are more of them!" I told Eddie as I frantically watched him search around for the key.

"I know!" he said as he reached for his wallet. He always kept a spare motorcycle key on him. "Found it!" he said as he pulled out the key.

My eyes swept around for any sign of the beasts, and I saw them. One of my paintings was leaning up against one pile of boxes. I forgot everything that Eddie had told me about gargoyles and did the most stupid thing ever. I ran to get them.

"Shelly, no!"

I could almost touch the paintings with my fingertips. I was so close to them. That's when I felt razor-sharp stone talons dug deep into my back. I tumbled flat on my face. *This is the end*, I thought.

"Duracell!" my friend shouted as a blue ball of energy knocked the gargoyle off my back and into the air.

I managed to roll out of the way as I heard Eddie bellow, "Nebulae!" I watched in numb amazement as a giant ball of fire hit the creature. It let out a scream of agony before its body blew up into dust. I lay in a pile of torn canvases and broken frames until the vampire picked me up in his arms and sprinted back to the motorcycle. He set me on the back seat and began to

unbutton his shirt. I was too dazed and in too much pain to read

his mind. He took off his shirt and threw it over my bleeding

back. I managed to slip my arms into the sleeves. Then we both

put on our helmets. At least our heads would be intact when the

gargoyles ate us. If we survived the motorcycle ride.

"Gargoyles can't smell covered blood," he told me as he

started up the motorcycle. "Hang on to me!"

I threw my aching arms around Eddie's bare chest.

Normally, this would have sent me to cloud nine, but because we

were being chased by two more gargoyles, I just hung on for

dear life as he gunned the motorcycle.

We sped past the quiet mansions filled with the sleeping

rich and famous. I looked at Eddie's side mirror and saw that

gargoyles were right on our tail. One by one, house lights

flickered on, illuminating the path we left behind.

Eddie made a sharp right on Main Street, the downtown

area of Zephyr. We raced down the road with the shrieking

beasts behind us. Drunks cursed us for waking them from their drunken stupors, and I counted at least five red lights that Eddie ran. Suddenly, he did a complete 180°, and we were facing our attackers. About five yards behind them was a thirty-foot brick wall that served as part of the downtown parking garage. "What are you doing?" I asked.

"Trust me, Shelly!" Eddie shouted back at me. Pushing the throttle all the way down, he sped right under the flying things and towards the brick wall.

I wanted to shut my eyes, but I was too scared to do anything. Instead, I pressed my cheek against his back, bracing for impact. A foot before we hit the wall, the motorcycle made a left sharp turn, tires screeching, and rubber burning. The other noise I heard was stone smashing against stone, I looked up just in time to see the second gargoyle collide at top speed into the wall. His whole body shattered, and he followed his brother to the ground in shambles.

Eddie pulled the bike to a stop. He turned around in his seat. "You can let go of me now."

I released him from my vice grip. "Sorry," I mumbled.

"It's all right. At least, we're safe."

"I wouldn't make any promises to her right now, Van Helsing!" We looked up to see a gargoyle, much larger than what we had seen so far, landing an only few feet away from us. Stregone slid off its back with a smug expression on his face. "I must say, Van Helsing, I'm impressed. You escaped from your bonds and defeated almost all of my gargoyles. I wonder if you can stop this!" He paused only for a moment before he screamed the word, "Duracell!" A blast of red energy about the size of Texas lifted the bike off the ground, and we went crashing against the wall. Then the world around me went black.

Chapter 12:
A Nice Ending for Some,
Not So Nice for Others

Nurses came in and out of my hospital room, thinking that I was still asleep. I vaguely remembered a police detective coming into my room and asking a series of questions relating to last night's events. But since I was all drugged up, I highly doubted my answers were very coherent. I had been awake for a few minutes, trying to establish my surroundings. I sank back on the white hospital pillow and shut my eyes to block out the sudden pain that shot up and down my back. I had forgotten about the talon marks in my back. When I wasn't slipping into unconsciousness from the anesthesia, I remembered the doctors saying that I fractured my shoulder. I reached up with my free arm and touched the bandage wrapped around my head. Nothing like a minor concussion to break the boredom of a Thursday night.

A few minutes later, Creighton came into my room in her nurse's uniform, carrying a bed tray loaded with a bowl full of green Jell-O and a glass bubbling over with ginger ale. "How are you feeling, Shelly?" she asked as she set the tray on the table with the mobile top. "Nice to see you awake."

"Okay, I guess!" I replied with a false smile. "What day is it?" I had no idea how long I had been asleep.

"Early Friday afternoon," she replied. The centaur looked up at the bouquet of white and purple striped roses that was sitting on a nearby table. "Who sent you the flowers?"

I looked over at the blue vase of flowers. When did they come in here? Then I vaguely remembered someone bringing them in awhile ago. "I think a nurse brought them earlier today. I can't really remember because I must have been zoning out at the time." I attempted to sit up with my good arm but failed miserably. "Can you see who they're from?" I asked.

Creighton parted some of the flowers but shook her head. "No card. Nothing!" She smiled at me. "It looks like you've got a secret admirer."

"Yeah, right, it's probably from my dad and Amelia or

Robin, and they forgot to sign a card."

"R-r-r-right," Creighton said. Suddenly, her pager went off. "Oops, got to go! I have to prep old Mr. Elfstone for his surgery."

I gave her a thumbs-up. "Have fun," I said as she left my room. "I'll be here. Eating my green Jell-O." I pulled the tabletop so that it hung over my bed. I finished about half of my ginger ale when I drifted off to sleep again.

I was watching television when I heard a knock on my door. "Come in," I said as if I really had a choice. I smiled the minute I saw my dad and his girlfriend come in carrying another bouquet of green and pink striped carnations. "Set them over there," I told Amelia, pointing to the sill where the mystery bouquet was.

Dad came over and kissed me on the forehead. "How are you feeling, sweetie?" he asked me.

"I'm in the hospital. I feel super!" I said with a lame smile.

Amelia shook her head full of short black hair. "At least, you weren't hurt any worse."

"I hope this is a lesson to you," Dad admonished playfully. "Always be careful on a motorcycle even if you are being chased by gargoyles."

"Hey," I asked, realizing that I wasn't the only person who was in the accident, "is Eddie okay?"

Amelia brushed back one of my bangs that had fallen out of the bandage. She was just like a mom to me, and I realized how much I've missed my own mother all these years. "Eddie's fine. You know vampires." She looked at me as if she knew all about my crush on Eddie. I wondered if Creighton had told her. "They heal quite fast."

My dad looked down at his cell phone. "The electrician just called about that faulty wiring. I'll take this outside. Get some rest, Shelly."

"I'll be along in a minute, Timothy," Amelia told him as he left the room. Once he was gone, she closed the door behind him with her mind. Then she came to sit down on the edge of my bed. "How long has your crush on Eddie been going on?"

"Creighton told you and Dad, didn't she?" I asked.

"Just me. Don't worry. Your secret's safe with me. She

thought that you might need someone else to talk with. Plus, I had already had put two and two together. Eddie had gone as your date to the art showing. You have been visiting him almost every night he's been working."

Thanks for spilling the beans, Creighton. I would have a talk with her later. Then I took a sip of my ginger ale. Nothing gets past Amelia. "I guess for a while. Why? You think that's bad that I like him?"

"Oh, no! Not at all! Eddie's a nice young man and a hard worker."

"What's the catch?" I narrowed my eyes at her.

"Well, Creighton mentioned you seemed afraid to tell him how you feel."

Was I that obvious? I needed to stop hiding my feelings. "Yeah, I guess so. It's kind of hard because he's one of my best friends. I'm afraid that if we aren't on the same page emotionally that we'll lose the great relationship we have."

"Are you on the same page?"

"Eddie said something last night about him caring about me a lot. But I think he meant more than just a friend."

"Did you try reading his mind?"

"He's cautious about his thoughts around me." Then I broke into a smile. "I have caught him thinking that I've looked hot or really nice in some outfits." I paused for a minute or two. "So, how did you know that Dad really liked you?"

"I asked him, but I was careful because I knew that he was a widower with two grown children."

"Yeah, you're widowed, too. Wouldn't that have made it easier to talk to him?"

"You see, when he moved down the street from me, I was just like you. I had a crush on him, but afraid of telling him how I felt. So, one day, the subject was brought up, and I told him how I felt. As it turned out, he was falling in love with me, too. And here we are."

"So, you're saying that I should tell Eddie how I feel about him, but I should wait for the right moment."

Amelia smiled at me. She bent down and kissed me on the forehead. "You'll know when it comes. Your father gave Eddie the night off. So, he might be coming by to see you tonight. Get some rest, Dear."

Subtle hint, Amelia, I thought but didn't say it. "Thanks for the flowers. I'll see you later." I waved goodbye to my dad's girlfriend as she left me with my thoughts.

Other people filtered in and out of my room for the next hour or two, asking how I was feeling over and over again. My next visitor happened to be Robin. He came in wearing street clothes. "How are you feeling?" he asked me.

"Guess," I replied irritably. I was tired of people asking me how I was feeling. Hello, I'm in a freaking hospital bed! "I'll give you a hint. My arm's in a sling, my back hurts, and I look like I have a turban wrapped around my head."

"So, how many times have you actually lied to your visitors?"

"I've lost count," I remembered the mysterious flowers and my brother's talent. "Did you send me those flowers?"

Robin shook his head. "No, why do you ask?" He headed over to the window sill and looked for a card. "It looks like you've got a secret admirer, and I think I know who they're from." He smirked at me before he answered. "I bet they're from Eddie."

"No, they're not!" I objected.

"You would *so* like it if they were," he teased. Even though he is only a year older than I am, my brother can be such a pain in the butt sometimes. Then his face lit up as if he remembered something. "Guess what?"

"What?"

"I got promoted! You're looking at Sergeant Robin Anderson!" he said as he grabbed both my shoulders excitedly.

"Robin," I replied through clenched teeth, "let go of my injured shoulder, please."

Robin immediately released me and held up his hands "Oh, sorry, Shelly!"

"Thank you!" I said. "Now, when did this happen?" Robin looked at me, blankly. "Your promotion, not my injured shoulder."

"After I arrested Mario Stregone for illegally owning gargoyles and hazardous use of magic. We found lots of evidence against him. He was selling protein drinks made out of illegal blue mushrooms. And we also have evidence of where the missing case files on him went and that Detective Angus was taking bribes from him."

"Really?" I asked, feigning shock.

Robin crossed his arms. "Don't act surprised. Eddie told us everything last night."

So much for our little mafia secret. "So, are we in trouble?" I asked Robin. "Because technically we weren't breaking into his house. Stregone did tell us that his house was my house."

Robin sighed. "Your justification scares me. Considering everything that happened, there were no charges filed against you or Eddie. But Shelly, I've to ask you one question: Why did you crash a mob boss's party?"

I grinned sheepishly. "Because I'm an idiot."

"Well, at least, Eddie was there to help you." He checked his watch. "I have to meet the guys at Strider's." The "guys" included Dirk, Tucker, and Strider. They are a part of his band that he hadn't come up with a name for yet.

"Maybe this practice, you'll come up a name for your band," I said. At one time, I had suggested to Robin the name the *Ungrateful Dead*, and his response was, "Go jump in a lake!"

"Whatever!" Robin said. "Get well soon, sis!" he waved

good-bye to me and left.

The clock on my hospital room wall read 7:30p.m. I was eating a spoonful of the Zephyr General Hospital's equivalent of Spam when there was a knock on my door. "Come in," I said. I think my heart rate skipped a couple beats when the vampire came in with a large, brown bag in his hand. "Hey, Eddie!" I said, trying to contain my excitement.

He took one look at me. "God, you look like crap!" he said honestly as he pulled up a chair next to my bed.

"At least you're honest 'cause that's exactly how I feel!" I held out my plate to the vampire. "Care for some dry and tasty mystery meat? And for dessert, blue Jell-O!"

Eddie grimaced. "I think I'll pass on getting my stomach pumped, thank you. Hospital food is one of the reasons why I'm a vegetarian."

"I'm with you there," I said as I sat up with Eddie's help. "You'd think that in a magical land filled with vampires, werewolves, satyrs, elves, and fairies, that they could make decent hospital food!"

"Well, there's no such thing as a perfect world."

I smiled at him. "So, what happened after I blacked out?"

Eddie gave me a fanged smile. "Well, I would be lying to you if I said that I blasted Stregone away with my nebulae spell. Instead, the police showed up and arrested him and his cronies. I did tell your brother everything. I hope you're not mad at me."

I shrugged with my good shoulder. Heck, as if I could've done anything while I was blacked out. "No, I'm not mad. Just glad that everything worked out, I guess."

The vampire's face suddenly became solemn. He opened the bag that he had set on the floor and pulled out my three paintings.

I stared in absolute amazement as I realized that I was looking at the undamaged prints. The last time that I had seen them was when that gargoyle had destroyed them. "Eddie, what happened?" I asked after a few minutes of stunned silence. "How did you fix them?"

"I took them to a wizard who was able to repair them," he replied, his voice beginning to choke with emotion. "It was the least I could do."

In my injured state, I realized that something was deeply troubling my friend. "Eddie, what's wrong?"

"Look, Shelly," he replied, his voice quivering with raw emotion. "It's my own stupid fault that you nearly got killed! If I hadn't been such an idiot, you wouldn't be in this blasted hospital bed!"

"Well, I shouldn't have gone back for the paintings," I replied.

"Shelly, you don't understand how worried I've been about you since Stregone attacked us with his energy spell!"

I sat back in stunned silence as I realized what Eddie meant. Reading his real emotions, he felt entirely responsible for my injuries, even though it was my idea to invade the mob boss' party. He really cared for me, but not just as a friend.

"Shelly, I've really screwed up these past few weeks, but I never meant for you to get hurt. Can you ever forgive me?"

"Of course, I will, Eddie. I know that you never meant for this to happen. Things just got out of control, but I made it out alive, thanks to you." I looked directly into his eyes. "You did some pretty amazing things the other night."

Eddie blushed, relieved that we were back on good terms again. He looked over at the mystery bouquet. "I see you got my flowers."

Dang it! Robin was right! I hate it when my brother is right. I would never hear the end of it. "They're really beautiful. Thanks, Eddie."

"Did you read the card?"

"What card?"

Eddie got up from his seat and looked hurriedly around the flowers. "It must have dropped on the way here. I'm sorry!" he apologized as he sat back down.

"What did it say?" I asked, trying to contain my excitement. Was this the moment Amelia had told me to look out for? I didn't want to be presumptuous, so I decided not to read his mind. I leaned forward with anticipation.

"I can't remember," my friend flat-out lied. I think he was blushing a bit.

"Oh!" I said as I racked my tired brain. I needed to come at him from another angle. Finally, I had it. "Eddie, when we were still handcuffed, did you mean all those things you said about caring for me?"

"Yeah! Of course, I did. Look, Shelly, I do care about you, not just as a friend, but—."

"But what?" I asked maybe a little too excitedly.

"Look, I like you more than a friend, but I'm not sure how you feel about us."

"I like the thought of us—together. I think we have a future."

"Me too, Shelly," Eddie said in a gentle, soft voice that I had never heard him use before. He leaned over and tenderly caressed my cheek. "Me, too."

COMING SOON

Yard Sale of the Undead

*My Life Among the Undead:
Book 2*

Being a librarian, Shelly Anderson has seen some strange things inside books. When a spider falls out of a book on natural disasters, she barely bats an eye. She has more important things to worry about. How is she going to convince her father that her vampire boyfriend, Eddie Van Helsing, is trustworthy? And how is she going to open up a portal to her old universe to rescue her childhood friends from danger when the only superpower she has is telepathy? To make matters worse, that same spider has turned into a gigantic, B-movie creature. Now, it's up to Shelly and Eddie to stop the dangerous arachnid before it completely destroys the city of Zephyr.

ABOUT THE AUTHOR

Like Shelly, Camara M. Bragdon is a librarian at her local library in Maine. Unlike Shelly, she is not a telepath, which she considers a blessing. When she is not writing, you can find her reading, antiquing, watching crime shows, or mastering Mahjong Tiles.